TWO ANGELS

NIVEDITA VEDURLA

INVINCIBLE PUBLISHERS

First published in India in 2017 by Invincible Publishers

ISBN: 978-93-87328-07-5

Invincible Publishers

G-120, Sushant Lok III, Sector 57, Gurugram-122002

Opposite Kasturba Ashram, Radaur Distt. Yamuna Nagar
Haryana-135133

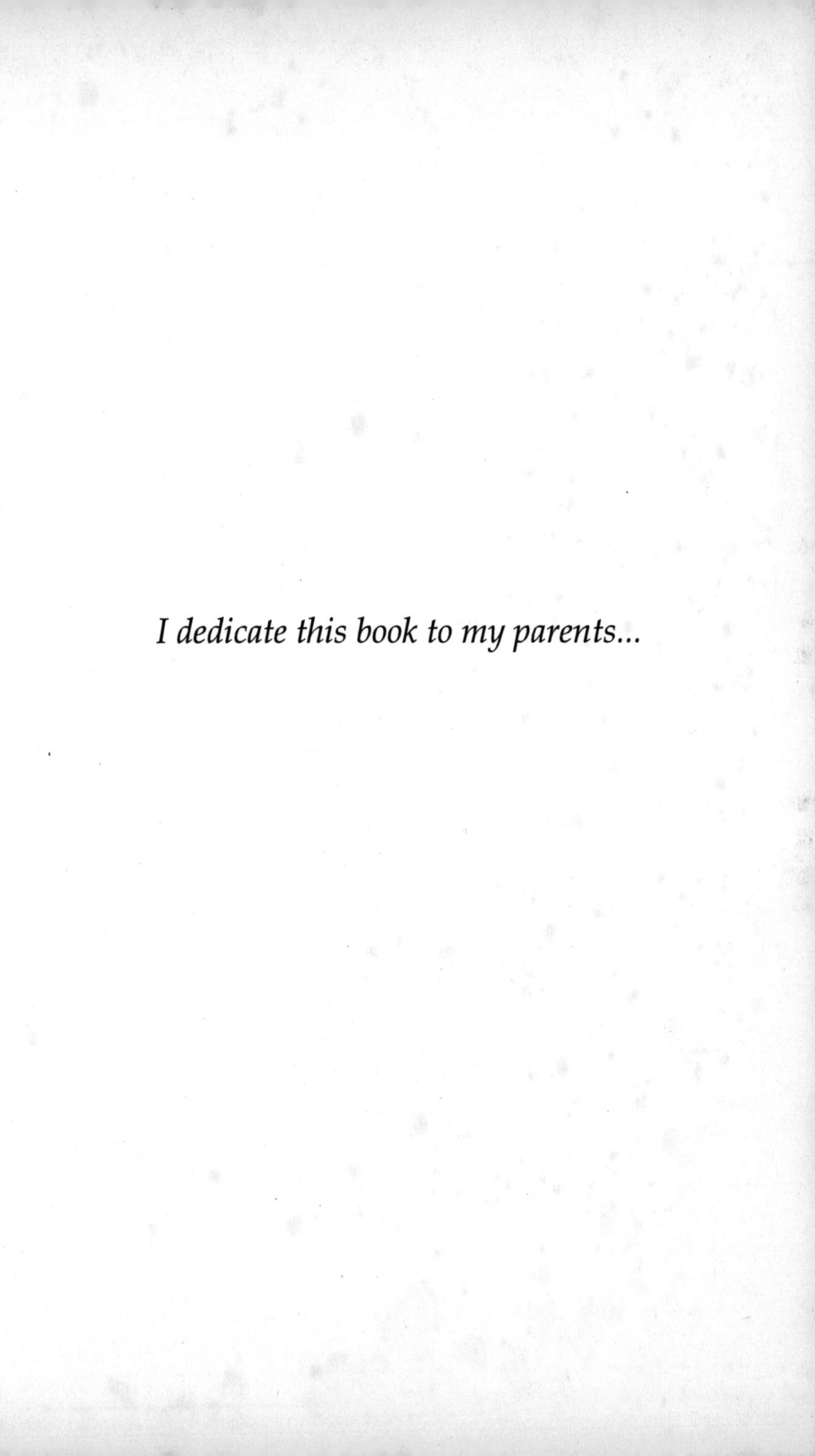

I dedicate this book to my parents...

ACKNOWLEDGEMENT

I wasn't able to express love in words till I became a mother. Words started pouring out as I began experiencing love more closely. This story of Arun and Esha is the first that I have written with a desire to explore the love and affection we long for from each relationship that we have.

This journey of writing a love story has made me thankful for love in all its forms that the Almighty has blessed me with.

My parents' constant support and motivation has made me the person I am today. I believe I have inherited my father's stint for storytelling, which has made me the writer the I am. My mother's constant support gave me everything I needed in life. In Suvasish Ranjan Sahoo, I found my husband, my best friend, my better half, and I have grown from his love. I wake up every day to find joy and inspiration in my son. My family and friends keep me going, and I thank each one of them.

To keep this book going it took a bit of searching to find the people I needed. A special thank you to Anuradha Kapoor, for her advice, encouragement, and friendship along the way. I am thankful to Tammanna Aurora, my Editor, for being ever so enthusiastic and giving her best.

Love is a powerful, transformative force and I hope each of you experiences the magic.

Prologue

That December morning, the city woke up to an unusually cold weather. There was a gathering stillness; the trees unmoving, their leaves wrapped tightly to their branches, birds silenced of their chirruping, nestled close to each other for warmth.

The only movement was that of a sparrow, as small as a child's hand, with a dark patch at the center of its breast, perched on the window sill and pecking at the glass. It remained there in the cold for hours, waiting to be fed and patted on the back, but it was getting quite late now. With each passing minute, the bird lost hope and its shrill chirps grew quieter. It was noon by the time it finally gave up and flew away, while Esha had still not risen out of bed.

The harsh cold had seeped into the house. All the flower decorations, photographs and candles in the room suddenly appeared shorn of all warmth or meaning. Arun watched the disappointed sparrow fly away without really seeing it. He held Esha's left hand and looked down at her still form, lost in deep sleep on the bed. Their dog Rambo lay beside the bed, his chin resting on the floor and his misty eyes locked on Esha.

Her beautiful face was pale and her eyes peacefully shut. 'She could be dreaming with that hint of a smile on her dry pink lips,' he thought. "Esha," he called out with a broken voice. Tears glazed his cheeks. She did not move in the slightest to his call. He knew she would not get up to stroke his hair or give him a pleasant smile and say, "Good morning, love." It was not going to happen that day, nor the next day, nor ever there after. Yet his heart was not ready to let the thought sink in that she had left the world.

The Doctor had confirmed late the previous night that Esha was no more. He had sat beside her and refused to leave her even for a minute. He had looked at her all through the night, praying constantly for any movement at all, perhaps even just a twitch, a smile or a word from her. His prayers had not been heard for dawn arrived and she still lay cold, unmoving and smiling ever so slightly. Every time someone came into the room to persuade him that he needed to let go, he pushed them away with all the revolting force he could muster. It was too soon for him to be able to comprehend all that had happened. He did not let anyone come close to his Esha. He had decided to not leave her hand, come what may.

Arun's mother cried all night, watching him from the doorway. She knew that this wasn't what Esha would have wanted. Finally she moved towards her son, stroked his hair and held him close to her chest. Arun allowed himself to be enveloped in his mother's embrace, but kept a tight hold on

Esha's hand regardless. After several minutes, she took his head in between the soft palms of her hands and made him look at her. "She suffered for two months. She had been stuck in bed and wracked constantly with pain, unable to even sleep at night. Doctors had given her so many injections, pierced her entire body searching for veins. She struggled through each moment and yet, she smiled for us. Did you want her to suffer more? Did you really want her to have stayed and smiled for the sake of your happiness, while she suffered from within. Don't you love her enough to let her go and rest in peace?"

These last few words of his mother rang in Arun's ears, finally making him realise what he had been doing. Slowly, he turned his head back towards Esha and took a moment to look at and appreciate every detail of her face. He then laid her hand back down on the bed carefully. As soon as he let her go, he broke down completely.

Arun weeped, loud and long, till his lungs couldn't sustain his grief anymore. It sounded as though his cries would reach the skies and plead with God himself for Esha's life back. Arun's mother led him away, out of the room. She gestured to the others to get Esha ready for the last rites. She had given particular instructions that Esha was to be dressed in her favourite light pink, layered dress that Arun had gifted her. They were to place Arun's letters beside her and decorate her coffin with blue orchids and white lilies.

A somber procession headed towards the Church's graveyard. Arun sat blankly through the prayers and barely heard the priest give his blessings. When the time came to bury Esha's coffin, he started to get unstable again. He tried to stop the burial and had to be held back physically by friends and relatives. When they released him, he fell to the ground and started digging with his hands. He gave up after a few tries, clutching handfuls of soil and falling back in despair. The relatives watched him struggle in silence, their eyes full of pain and sympathy.

During the ceremony, Arun's mother heard whispers taking rounds, "Such a young girl, so pretty, so kind. Why did she have to get this disease? Poor Arun, how is he going to survive without her? They didn't have any children." These words struck at her heart like sharp nails. Yet, what they said was the bitter truth. She knew that Esha's sudden death had created a huge vacuum in Arun's life and that he would have to fight this emptiness all alone. She could do nothing to ease the pain of Esha's absence or to fill the gap that she had left behind in his life.

She silently stood near Esha's burial ground, with eyes moist and her heart heavy. She felt it was hopeless to pray to God for her son because God never listened to her prayers for Esha's recovery in the first place. All she could do was to pray to Esha's soul to give them some sign of hope so that Arun could survive his unbearable loss.

No one could understand Arun's pain better than his mother and Esha herself. She placed a half-bloomed white rose on the ground and lit a candle.

Before

Chapter 1

Arun's father was at the peak of his career, managing multiple divisions of his company, when he got transferred to Mumbai. Yearly transfers to different states for work had become a regularity for him and his family.

On the first day of his new school, Arun watched his mother pack his superman-sticker'd tiffin box with delicious food, the way she always did for every first day at a new school. He knew it wasn't his fault, but it felt like a punishment to start from scratch almost every year. Deep within his heart, he hated it. Arun's mother chattered away happily around the house, but Arun couldn't bring himself to say anything. Looking up at him, she asked, "What's the matter? Why the sad face? Aren't you excited about your new school?"

"What should I be excited for? Next year Dad will get

another transfer. I will have to join another school, lag behind on the syllabus and struggle making new friends all over again," Arun grumbled and slumped down on the couch.

Arun's mother came to sit next to him. Stroking his head gently, she said, "I understand it is tough to make new friends and adjust to a new school over and over again, but who knows, you might find very good friends here and have a really good time at this school. You should see life as a learning experience and not complain about it."

He listened to her carefully, but didn't respond. She patted his back and continued, "You know what, I have a good feeling about this place. This school and the friends you make here will be the best."

Lifting his head up, he looked at her with beaming eyes and asked, "Are you sure?"

She nodded her head, made him stand facing her, adjusted his tie and said, "Now get ready, you don't want to be late on your very first day!"

Despite his mother's reassurance, Arun was quiet on their way to St. John Missionary High School. His parents bid him goodbye at the Principal's office, following which, he put on a brave face and followed a teacher to the sixth standard classroom. Arun could hear the buzz of loud chatter, laughter, and giggles down the corridor, the walls of which were decorated with colourful sketches. When they reached the door of the classroom, the first person he saw was a short-haired girl, standing near the blackboard. Holding a chalk in hand, she was imitating the teacher. As soon as the students caught sight of the teacher at the door, they scurried back to their their wooden desks and fell silent. The girl turned around to face them timidly.

The teacher shouted, "Esha, what is going on here? I will definitely tell the principal about your mischief this time."

At once, Esha reached for her ears with chalk-powdered hands and flashed a bright smile, saying, "Sorry Ma'am! I will not do it again."

The teacher caught hold of Esha's ears, but Arun could see she was not really angry. Releasing her ear soon, she scolded, "You know very well how to use that big smile and say sorry. Now go sit down at your seat and I want no more trouble from you." He watched Esha skip back to her desk happily.

"Class! This is Arun," the teacher beckoned him forward. "He is new to the school and the city and I want you all to make friends with him. Esha, he will sit next to you. Arun has missed a number of lessons so help him with what has been covered so far in the syllabus. And see that you don't make him take on all your mischief!"

Adjusting his shirt sleeves, Arun walked quietly over to Esha's desk. He hung his bag at the back of his chair and sat down without making eye contact with anyone. The teacher left, and he could feel everyone's curious gaze shift onto him. Esha turned to him and smiled, "Hi Arun, welcome to our class."

Arun looked at her unkempt uniform, messy hair, chalk-powdered hands and reluctantly said hello.

Esha continued rapidly, "Which school were you in before coming here?"

Arun had grown tired of this question and let out a heavy sigh. He was about to snap a reply, but then he remembered his mother's words about this school being the best for him. He replied politely, "I was in Little Buds School in Allahabad. My father just got transferred to Mumbai so I joined this school."

Esha opened her mouth to ask more, but the class teacher entered just then for the next lesson and everybody stood up saying, "Good afternoon, Sir." Arun remained quiet all through the class. He made no effort to talk to anyone. He paid complete attention to the teacher and wrote sincerely in his notebook.

An hour later, the bell rang for break and Arun sighed with relief. He was finding it difficult to keep up with all the new lessons. Everybody jumped up from their seats and collected into small separate groups. He watched everyone play, talk and eat their tiffins together. Nobody paid any attention to him. He reached into his bag and took out his superman sticker'd tiffin box. He found the lid of the box too tight. He applied all the force he could muster and it opened with a jerk, slipping out of his hand. He looked at the mess on the ground in dismay. 'This day just keeps getting worse,' he thought. He picked up the soiled food and looked around for a dustbin.

That's when he noticed Esha watching him. She looked sympathetically at him and pointed to the dustbin placed in one corner of the class. Arun's face turned red with embarrassment. He quickly tossed the food in and left the room to wash his hands. When he came back, Esha was waiting by their desk for him. She offered her tiffin to him and said, "Why don't you share mine?"

Arun shook his head and said, "No, thanks."

"Don't worry, my mother always makes extra food for me. We can share," Esha insisted.

Arun shook his head again, but Esha was persistent. Finally, he took a small piece reluctantly and placed it in his mouth. Esha smiled and placed the tiffin at the center of the wooden table for them to share.

Watching them so, two other people came up and offered to share their food as well. Arun was hesitant, but Esha kept smiling and encouraging him. Arun watched how Esha mingled and talked to everyone. She was always teasing and smiling. Arun felt shy sitting in a group where so much attention was on him. Esha and the others, Rohit and Priyanka, kept asking him questions and told him stories about their school.

By the time the school day ended, Arun was still not

comfortable with everyone being so friendly. When Arun's mother came to pick him up, he was happy to be going home, but he felt even happier waving back at his three new friends and talked non-stop the entire journey back.

The next couple of weeks passed by quickly. Arun did not adjust right away. He was not used to an extroverted nature as that of Esha's and often watched her quietly as she cheerfully greeted everyone, offered her tiffin, talked, helped, laughed, and played. He would often just give a small nod or say hi, and then sit quietly for most of the day. He was still having a hard time going through his books, not knowing which sections had already been covered. When a teacher asked the class to open the section that she had taught previously, he just looked at the teacher confusedly. At such instances Esha would smile and quickly help him locate the correct page.

Arun noticed that Esha was making an effort to help him out with small things. The very first day, she had whispered the names of teachers and their subject to him at the beginning of each period. Since then she had been making jokes and imitating them every day. Arun couldn't help but laugh and admire Esha's naughtiness. She was also a smart girl, he soon realised. She knew the answers to all the questions and did not mind sharing them with Arun so that he could keep up with the lessons too.

First he thought she was being kind because the teacher had asked her to help him. But she did not leave his side even during lunch breaks and included him in all their games. It became a routine where Esha would open her tiffin and offer it to Arun first. He would shy away and say No thanks, I have mine, and she would insist, Try a bite, at least.

He had the best experience travelling by the school bus for the first time. Arun's mother had encouraged him to start taking the bus. Arun knew that his mother wanted him to spend more time with his new friends. He entered the bus with trepidation, but almost immediately heard Esha's voice shouting his name. She was sitting in the back with Rohit and Priyanka. She scooted aside to make place for Arun. He was surprised at her gesture and sat down beside her. From then on, she always kept place next to her reserved for him. One day, Arun came to the realisation that the four of them had formed a group amongst themselves.

He slowly opened up to his friends and started enjoying school. He had never had friends like this where they did their homework, chatted and played together. The four of them were always laughing, teasing, cracking jokes, munching on snacks, telling stories, discussing school topics, and singing songs with each other. Their talks were endless as they shared their thoughts on every conceivable thing on the planet. All the time in the world still fell short for their gossip!

Arun and Esha's bond, which had been so special from day one, was cemented strong the day she celebrated Arun's success without even a hint of hurt or jealousy. They had started participating in debates and quiz competitions and enjoyed a healthy rivalry. Inevitably, they faced each other in a competition while representing two different houses of their school. Arun's group won the debate while Esha's team lost poorly. Waiting outside afterwards, Arun was skeptical about Esha's reaction, but then he saw her walking towards him with a wide smile on her face.

As soon as she reached close to him, she extended her hand towards him and said, "Congratulations, Arun." Arun did not know what to say and thanked her gently. Paying no attention to his sad face and low voice, she pointed to an ice cream vendor near the school's main gate and said, "Arun, you'll have to treat me to ice-cream for winning the competition!"

Arun was thrilled to see Esha happy for his win. He grabbed her hand, tugged her towards the school gate and said, "Yes, let's go and have it!"

It soon became a tradition between them. Whenever one of them won anything, they would run to tell the other person, and then they would have ice cream together.

Three years later, when Arun stood first in the final exams of class nine, they celebrated once again with ice cream. He often wondered how he got so lucky to have a best friend like Esha. Topping the class was a special achievement for him. Arun knew that Esha deserved half the credit for helping him study. 'If I could, he would have bought her all the ice cream in the world,' he thought to himself, as they said goodbye that day.

Arun rushed inside his house, bursting to show the results to his mother, knowing how happy she would be to see his achievement. When he found her in the sitting room with her head bent down, he knew immediately that something significant had happened. The usual light atmosphere of the house was fraught with tension that day. 'I will show her my result and make her smile,' he thought.

Quickly, he pulled out his mark sheet from his bag and jumped onto the couch next to her, "Ma, look!"

Arun's mother smiled with glittering eyes as soon as she saw the result, just as he predicted she would. She hugged Arun tight in her arms and said, "I'm so proud of you."

Just then, his father walked into the room and came over to see what the sudden excitement was about. He took the card from Arun's mother's hand, assessed it closely and patted Arun on the back. "Well done, Arun. Your results are excellent. This makes me very happy and I know you will work just as hard for your board exams next year," he said.

Arun's blushed at the reaction of his parents, but he noticed that the worried expression had not entirely left their faces. Reclining back on the sofa, Arun's father stroked Arun's hair gently and said in a soft voice, "We have some big news to tell you. I have been transferred to Nagpur. Your mother and I have decided however, that this time I will go there alone, and both of you will stay here till you finish your schooling. Now, I know you are a grown-up, and I think you are responsible enough to take care of yourself and your mother."

Arun was taken aback. He was not ready for this. He opened his mouth to convey his disagreement, but his mother started, "Arun, we know you have made good friends here, and class ten exams are very important for your future. We don't want your studies to get disturbed at this stage. Don't worry, your father will visit us every month."

Arun knew she was only trying to console him. 'It would be too hard for her to be away from dad herself,' Arun thought. He wanted to make her smile. He cast his eyes down and nodded his head. "I will miss you, Dad." He then hugged him and said, "I will do my best and work very hard."

Arun's mother wept, not being able to control herself anymore. Arun leaned over to wipe her tears away and kissed her cheeks.

The next day, he was uncommonly subdued on the bus to school. All his friends asked him what had happened. He told them about his father's transfer and how they had decided that he would stay in Mumbai with his mother. His friends didn't seem to understand why he was sad. He should be happy that he was getting to stay in Mumbai, they said.

Only Esha understood the pain in Arun's sad voice. She rested her hand on his shoulder and said, "Your parents are making this sacrifice for your own future. You must appreciate their effort and support this decision. You should help your mother and take care of her since your father will not be around. Cheer up now and make sure you give your best in your studies!"

Arun was glad for her motivation, and looked up at her with a watery smile. 'Esha is right. I have always been an obedient son, and now I have to step up and help my parents make the best of this situation,' he thought. Arun was determined to make them proud.

Arun's father left for Nagpur ten days later. Arun tried to take on all the chores that his father usually took care of; going out to make bill payments, helping with grocery shopping and making his mother tea and breakfast on Sundays.

It was not an easy year for him with advanced studies and all the extra responsibilities, but his friends supported him. Esha helped him study, Rohit accompanied him on errands, and together with Priyanka, they found time to play cricket, cycle, participate in competitions, go fishing and have fun.

It was mid-April before he knew it, and he found himself awaiting his board results. His friends had already started deciding on subjects for higher secondary, while some started applying to different schools and colleges. Arun, meanwhile, had a far more important decision to make. He was confused whether to continue studying in Mumbai or move to Nagpur? His father had been staying away from them for the past year and though his parents didn't show it, he could sense the problems they were facing in staying apart, visible through the pain in his mother's eyes.

He knew that his parents would never ask it of him, but he had to make the right choice. He did not want to be the reason for his family staying apart in two different cities. He did all the research himself and applied to a school in Nagpur. When it was time to tell everyone, the guilt of leaving his friends was only overcome by seeing his parents' happiness.

On the last day of school, he walked home feeling sad about all the impending goodbyes. Arun's mother however, had arranged a surprise for him. He found all his friends were waiting for him at his house, when he got back.

"I know how special these friends are to you and how much you will miss them. So today, celebrate and have fun!" she said, ruffling his hair fondly.

Arun was overjoyed at their last get-together. All of them stuffed themselves full on delicacies, wrote about each other in their slam books and played in the park till it got dark. When it was time to leave, Arun became sad again. Rohit's eyes got moist too as he said, "We will all miss you, Arun."

Next to him, Esha started to cry. Arun did not know what to say. He realised how difficult is was going to be to not meet her every day. Arun's mother came over and hugged Esha tight. "You are all such good friends, I am sure you will keep in touch and meet again," she said, comforting Esha.

Arun watched Esha leave with a heavy heart. As he waved goodbye, he wondered when they would meet again.

Chapter 2

Arun's first day of class eleven in Nagpur did not go smoothly at all. That morning brought with it the usual rush of getting ready, trying to leave on time and dealing with nerves over starting at a new school all over again. In all that confusion, he forgot to take his new school ID card with him. It was only when he reached the school gate and the guard stopped him that he realised he had forgotten the card at home.

"Give me your name and wait outside. I will have to arrange for a temporary card for you," said the guard, giving him a cold stare.

Cursing himself, Arun moved to stand aside, next to a few others boys. He glared at the banner in front of him which had the names of toppers who had gone on to study at

IIT's. Dejectedly he thought, 'First days at new schools have never been good for me and this time there will be no Esha to sit next to, either.'

"Hi, I am Pratik," a voice broke the chain of his thoughts. Arun turned out to find a tall boy with curly hair, smiling at him and a hand extended towards him for a handshake. Arun reluctantly pulled his right hand out of the pocket and shook hands with him.

"Did you forget your I-Card too?" asked Pratik. Barely waiting for him to answer, he continued, "I kept it on the table last night but this morning, I don't know how, I just forgot to pick it up."

Before Pratik could say anymore, the guard called them over. Together they walked inside, collected the temporary I-Card, and headed towards the auditorium as it was instructed at the notice board. Pratik chatted away, but Arun was only half listening to him. He wondered what would happen next, how different this school would be from the one back in Mumbai and whether he would be able to make any good friends here.

The auditorium was quite a big one with staircase rows. Arun headed towards the last row of seats, but Pratik dragged him over to the middle. Pratik knew some of the other science students there and started talking to them. Arun stayed quiet, gently tapping his fingers over the books in his hand and feeling a little lost with so many new people around. He listened to the others talk and observed everybody in the auditorium as they settled in.

Almost half an hour passed before anybody entered. The big wooden doors at the back of the auditorium swung open and few students wearing a different uniform came in. They were clearly the seniors of that school. Arun watched them as they walked past him, joking with each other and rudely question the students in the front row, laughing and teasing them. They started to pick people then to come to the stage and introduce themselves, while they made fun of them.

Arun quickly ducked his face down and tried not to move. He wanted to stay as calm as possible so that no one would notice him. But as his luck would have it, he was called up to the stage. Trembling, he moved out of his seat and towards the front. He could feel the sweat under his shirt, trickling down his back. He had never spoken in front of such a large audience. And now he was about to get mocked and insulted for it too.

Gathering all his strength, he pulled himself up straight and wiped his forehead with a handkerchief. He paused for a second and said, "My name is Arun Shetty…."

'Maybe this wouldn't be so bad,' he thought. Suddenly, one of the seniors with a strip of blonde dyed hair jumped forward, startling him. Arun apprehensively watched him come closer. The senior remarked aloud, "Hey, it is our very own Mr. India. Everyone, welcome him with a applause…

hey, where did he go? I can't see him!"

Everybody started laughing. Emboldened by the cheer, the senior pushed forward and started unbuttoning Arun's shirt. Arun struggled and tried to stop him, but the senior had the advantage of being bigger in stature than him and managed to take his shirt off. Throwing Arun's shirt on the floor, he cheered, "Now I can see him. So, our Mr. India is visible when he doesn't wear his shirt."

Arun was humiliated and was driven close to tears. He knew well that they were mocking Anil Kapoor's character from the movie Mr. India, in which he had a device that made him invisible. Arun liked that movie, and had watched it several times, but in that one moment he hated it. He picked up his shirt and pushed past the seniors.

Before the seniors could do anything, a teacher came in, holding a few books and wearing a stern expression. He must have sensed from the scene that some form of ragging was taking place because he shouted angrily at the seniors, "What is all this going on? Why are you all here? If you don't behave properly, you will be thrown out of this school."

The seniors took it as their cue to leave and hurried out of the auditorium. Arun climbed up to his row, slipped back in his seat and tried not to make eye contact with anybody. Pratik gave him a sympathetic look, but said nothing. Arun was glad he did not have to speak.

The torture did not end there. With every passing day,

Arun disliked his school in Nagpur more and more. Every time the seniors passed by Arun's class, they would shout and say, "Mr. India, we are watching you." And if there was no teacher, they would enter the class and mess with him too.

He felt disturbed and did not know how he could change things. His classmates were not very friendly towards him either because they did not want to get on the bad side of the seniors. He often spent his days alone, thinking about his easy friendship with Esha. She would have known what to do, he thought. But since he had come to Nagpur, even she seemed to have deserted him. She had not called him even once, and there had been no reply to his emails.

Arun was frustrated to the core. His pain could be seen clearly on his face. He stopped going to school and stayed home for two days, giving the excuse of not being well. He started remaining angry and irritated all the time, and his mother noticed this change in his behaviour. The third day, when Arun tried to skip school again, she sat him down and asked, "What is going on, son? Is everything alright? You seem to be annoyed and worried about something."

Arun couldn't keep up the pretence anymore. He put down the TV remote and sighed, "Why did you name me Arun? Everybody makes fun of me. I don't like Nagpur. Let us move back to Mumbai."

Arun's mother caressed his back lovingly and said, "Your father named you after your grandmother, Arundhati Shetty.

However, I don't think getting teased about your name should make you so angry that you stop going to school. Have you forgotten how many times you have been teased by your friends back in Mumbai? You never became sad then, or angry. So, what is bothering you so much here?"

Arun held his head up, pursed his lips thinking about those moments and said, "Yes, I am not one to take a little teasing to heart, but I don't like staying here, especially because the people here are not good. They behave so rudely with me. Every time they see me, they make fun of me."

Arun's mother listened carefully and deduced correctly, "So, they are ragging you."

"Yes, Ma," replied Arun, "I can't even complain about them. It will make things worse. Even my classmates don't want to be friends with me because of that."

Arun's mother shook her head and said, "Arun, life is not so easy. It will not give you roses every time. Sometimes, it will be bad and sometimes, it will even tear you to pieces, but you should always have hope. Remember, God is always with you, in good times as well as bad. Trust him always. Things will be easier to handle if you have trust in him."

Arun listened carefully to his mother's words. He was glad to have told her. She always had the wisdom to push him along. However, he still had no clue what to do about the situation. In a small voice he asked, "But what should I do now? I feel completely lost."

To his surprise, his mother smiled. "Ask someone to take a picture the next time the seniors tease you and then drop it at the principal's office."

He did not understand how it would help, but his mother told him to just trust her and sent him off to school the next day. Arun decided to seek out Pratik who came closest to be considered as his friend at that place. Arun explained how difficult things had become for him and insisted that it was time that he stood up for himself. It took a lot of persuasion on Arun's part and complete assurance that Pratik would not get caught, before he agreed to help.

They got a chance to put the plan in action that morning itself, when the seniors came to bother Arun again during the lunch break. Even while he was being pushed around by them, he kept an eye on Pratik taking the photographs.

The next day, Arun was called to the Principal's office. He entered nervously to find that the seniors had also been summoned. The Principal got straight to the point and asked, "Were they ragging you?"

Arun considered his options for a moment. This was his chance to complain about everything they had done to him. He looked towards the seniors standing on the other side. The one who had unbuttoned his shirt brought his index finger to his lips and shook his head. Another mouthed sorry.

The principal repeated his question impatiently, clasping both his hands over the table.

“No, sir,” said Arun, his heart beating fast.

“Can you explain why then is he holding your shirt?” Asked the Principal, holding up the photograph.

Arun quickly replied, “I was unaware that my shirt’s button was open. He had come to our class to meet his cousin. When he passed by, he noticed that my shirt was open and buttoned it.”

Arun was sure the Principal saw clearly through his lie. The Principal kept staring at him for a few seconds with a frown on his face. Finally he said, “If they rag you again, come straight to my office. I will punish them properly.”

Arun let out a short breath, nodded a thank you and followed the seniors out of the Principal’s office.

Once outside, the seniors turned to him, clapped him on the back and smiled. One of them said, “Thanks, Arun. That was really decent of you. You come to us if you face any trouble in school, okay?”

Arun smiled in relief and shook hands with them. While walking back to class, he felt like he was breathing properly for the first time.

From then on, Mr. India became his nickname and he laughed along when anyone mentioned it. His newfound friendship with the seniors made him hugely popular. He surrounded himself with his classmates, played games with them and studied sincerely. He no longer felt a yearning for Esha or his other friends in Mumbai. By the time class twelfth started, he had decided that perhaps Nagpur wasn't such a bad place after all.

Chapter 3

'I have become a robot,' Arun despaired, as he sat in a local train, sandwiched between people, waiting for his station. It was a hot summer evening, and he was sweaty and hungry. Work, eat, sleep, repeat; that had become his daily routine. Everyone had told him that this was the struggle for success and that he had to be prepared for it, but nobody warned him about the loneliness.

A year ago, he finished his engineering and came to Mumbai for his first job. It took him only a month to realise that life in the city was nothing like he remembered. His carefree childhood days seemed like a dream. This time, he stayed as a paying guest in a small apartment by himself near the railway station. Here, he did not have his mother with her unconditional love, her appetizing food, and the liveliness she brought to the house. He felt miserably alone.

For the first few days at the new guest house, the rattling sound of trains made him uneasy and the knocking in his head kept him up most nights. On these nights, he often thought about Esha and of getting in touch with her. He no longer had her contact however, and did not even know if she still lived in Mumbai. 'It has been so many years, what would we even talk about,' he wondered.

Instead, he threw himself into his work. The work stress was unending and often compelled him to work late into the night. This hectic life left him neither with time, nor the inclination to socialize. The only people he knew in the city anymore were his colleagues. His interaction with them was limited to lunchtime talks about the projects they were working on. Whenever he tried to initiate a casual conversation, he found the discussion turning into gossip about who is doing what, who is closest to which boss and why such and such person is getting a good bonus.

This office politics and gossip irritated him. Being ambitious and hardworking, he did not like to waste his time in such games. His dedication paid off, when at the end of the first quarter, he was given a promotion and was asked to take on the responsibility of training new recruits. That is how he met Rhea.

'I should have said something to her, congratulated her on such a good presentation at least,' thought Arun on his way home, weaving through the bustling crowd at the station, mentally berating himself for missing his opportunity.

Rhea stayed on his mind as he cooked chicken curry and steamed rice for dinner, while also when he ate it soon after. He felt a rush of adrenaline rising as he recalled the day she joined the company. She had arrived wearing a peacock blue dress, her eyes glittering, perfect red lips, and cheeks dusted with a tinge of pink. He knew he was not the only one drawn to her beauty. Even that very morning during the juniors' presentation, everyone had been charmed by her smile and beauty. She had on a sea green sari as she stood confidently in front of everybody and smiled so sweetly that Arun could hardly recall what she had said about the latest market trends in computer usage. Every time she had switched to a new slide projected on the wall, she tucked her long straight hair behind her ear and left him mesmerized.

He had wanted to say something to her, but he wasn't sure how to approach her. Everybody else present there during the presentation had gathered around her to congratulate her and Arun did not want to be just another face in the crowd. So he had walked away without anybody noticing him.

Getting into bed, he thought about Esha and how easily she had made friends with him. 'I should do the same with Rhea,' he mused with a soft grin. 'Tomorrow,' he decided, drifting off to sleep. 'Tomorrow I will go up to her and say hello.'

The next day, it was Rhea who approached him first. Arun was in the cafeteria finishing his coffee when Rhea appeared and sat down across from him. She smiled and said, "Hi Arun! How are you?"

Arun, taken by surprise, stammered, "I'm good, thank you. How are you? By the way, your presentation yesterday was very good."

"Thanks! If someone like you is appreciating it, then it must really have been good," she laughed, bringing a smile to Arun's face.

Arun placed his cup of coffee down and said mockingly amused, "Such importance for my opinion? I've never heard such a thing before."

"The most technically proficient of all, the apple of the seniors' eyes, is asking me why he is important," she replied, grinning from ear to ear.

"Stop giving me such false praises," blushed Arun, brushing the brim of the coffee cup.

He finished his coffee and looked at his watch. Reluctantly, he got up from the table and said, "I'll have to take your leave now. I have some important work to finish. I hope you will be comfortable alone. I will join you some other time."

To his pleasure however, Rhea also jumped up and said, "I'll head back with you, can't take such long breaks." She moved closer and fell into step beside him, as they walked back towards their desks.

Over the next few days he noticed that whenever he took a break, Rhea would be right behind him. She made sure to greet him every morning and tell him how smart he was looking, or how she admired his work. Not used to such praise, he always blushed and laughed it off. But her words often lingered in his mind. It started to make a difference to his personality and looks. He started paying attention to his clothes and how he did his hair. He started to spend more time with Rhea, going over to her desk at the end of each day to see if she needed any help.

One day, they were sitting at the cafeteria talking over coffee, when Rhea's senior Sumit joined them. He ate his snacks and talked loudly, commenting on some ongoing project and asked for Rhea's opinion on it. Arun could sense that Rhea felt a little uncomfortable. 'Perhaps I should leave and let them talk about their work,' he thought to himself. Aloud, he said, "I'll make a move now, have to finish my presentation. You guys continue."

Sumit turned around and said, "What is the time? I too have to send a list of new computers to the manager."

They were about to take their leave when Rhea reached out and pulled at Arun's arm. With a tense expression she said, "I need to talk to you about something."

Arun was taken aback by her behaviour. He looked over at Sumit and gestured to him to go ahead. To Rhea, he said,

"Yes, tell me what happened."

"I need help with the networking features to be embedded in the computers. The manager has asked me to complete it by tomorrow. I am finding it very difficult to do," she said making a sad face.

Arun smiled to see her so distressed over such a small thing. He said, "It is quite simple. I will explain it to you during lunch."

He felt Rhea place her hand on top of his and looked down. She said, "Thanks, you are very helpful Arun. But I won't be able to understand how to implement the code on my own. Will you come to my desk when you are free and help me with it?"

"What? Oh sure, I should be free by 5 P.M.. I have a meeting till 4:30, so I'll come over to help you after that," said Arun, finally making eye contact with her.

At that, Rhea squeezed his hand softly said, "Thanks a lot, Arun. That'll be perfect."

Arun walked back to his desk with a bright smile on his face. He was distractedly looking at some new emails on his computer when Sumit came over. He leaned against his desk, crossed his arms and asked, "So, what is going on, my friend?"

Arun was confused as to what Sumit was referring to. He looked up, hoping to figure it out from the expression on Sumit's face, but was unsuccessful. Curiously, Arun asked, "With my project, you mean?"

"With work?" mocked Sumit, "Back at the cafeteria…it looks like someone is getting close to you."

"Shut up, we are just friends. She needs my help adding networking features to the computers," said Arun with a quick smile and moved his attention back to his computer screen.

Sumit raised his eyebrows and said, "She could have asked me or someone else for it too. I think she likes you."

Arun had no response to that. He was left staring blankly at his computer screen after Sumit left. He thought about the moment when she had pulled at his arm to stop him from leaving. Something was definitely different; the way she talked, the way she smiled at him. 'Could Sumit be right?' he wondered.

The ping of a new email distracted him from these thoughts. He shook his head and murmured to himself that there was nothing going on and that they were just good friends which is why she had asked for his help. He felt convinced after this self-affirmation.

Exactly at 5 P.M., he headed over to Rhea's desk. She looked very pleased and relieved to see him. He tried to explain the code to her, but she was utterly confused. He asked her to step aside and took charge of the computer himself.

"Done," he said with a final click of the mouse about half an hour later.

Rhea clapped her hands, flashed a wide smile and exclaimed, "You are a champion with this coding stuff. You've got to teach me all this!"

Arun laughed at her excitement and said, "Of course, I will."

He couldn't help but smile, going back to his desk. Something seemed to have shifted between them. They really liked each other's company. The next day, Arun noticed that Rhea was less formal with him than usual. She patted his shoulder softly when greeting him and smiled at him saying, "Hi smarty, how are you today?"

Arun was flattered with her words. He busied himself with filling his glass with water and replied, "Good, good. What about you?"

"Nothing, just bored with work. It is no fun around here, except for the time I spend with you," said Rhea, grinning over the edge of her coffee mug.

She trailed after him, grabbing his left arm with her hand when he held the door open for her.

Arun was new to this experience. He had not realised that their casually intimate behaviour would attract a lot of attention. Rumours were already making rounds throughout the office. That afternoon, when Arun went to his manager's cabin for a usual work session review, he had a slight smile on his face and a spring in his step. The manager looked through his file and commented, “You have been with us for just six months and I already hear a lot of appreciation about your work from your seniors.”

“In fact,” he smirked and continued, “There is news that you have started liking the office a bit more ever since Rhea joined.”

Arun opened his mouth in surprise, but felt clueless as to what to say. Before he could manage a response, there was a knock on the glass door of the cabin.

The manager checked something off his notebook and said, “I have a meeting now with the board of directors. I will see you again at the end of this week. I have some additional responsibility to give you.”

Arun felt relieved that his manager did not have time to question him any further. He pushed his chair back and was almost out of the door, when the manager called out after him, “By the way Arun, I guess you should ask her out soon. There are too many in line, ready to do it if you don’t.”

These words from his manager echoed in his head all through the day. Arun had never done anything like it before, asking someone out. ‘Should I really ask her out? How should I do it?’ Arun bothered over how Rhea would react. ‘Surely, she likes me too,’ he thought. ‘I have to do something.’

The next day, Arun reached office a little early and placed

a big bouquet of red roses and a heartshaped card at Rhea's desk. For the next hour, he sat at his desk doing nothing, waiting for Rhea to arrive. Her laughter reached his ears even before he saw her. He quickly sat up straight in his chair and pretended to work on his computer. From the corner of his eye, he saw her come in wearing in a blue sleeveless dress. As she approach her desk, surprise grew in her eyes to see it all decked up. She bent down and retrieved the card first. 'Why does't she look happy?' Arun wondered nervously.

Rhea's face had turned red with anger. She marched right over to his desk and threw the card at him. "What do you think of yourself? Do you realise how cheap this looks?" she spat out furiously.

Arun was at a loss of words. Baffled at her reaction, he watched her walk away. Soon the bouquet arrived back at his desk too. He felt deeply humiliated. He could feel everybody's gaze on himself. He threw the card and the flowers in the dustbin and started stabbing at the keyboard in anger.

Three days went by and he started keeping to himself again, going back to his routine before Rhea had showed up in his life. He rarely visited the cafeteria after that, avoided Rhea completely, and concentrated solely on his work. At the end of the week, he went back to his manager's cabin, seeing the reminder notification flash at his outlook application. He hoped the manager would not mention the Rhea fiasco. Fortunately for him, the manager was busy and quickly assigned Arun his work.

It was the first happy moment for him that week. He was tasked with selecting the freshers who were to continue with the company and those who were going to be let off. The news quickly spread through the office and Arun overheard many people saying that he would use his newfound power to take revenge on Rhea.

However, he paid no heed to the gossip and went about his work as per procedure. When the appointment letters were handed out to the freshers, he watched Rhea sigh with relief, sitting on her desk. He did not want to think about her, so he packed up quickly and left for home.

There was an e-mail waiting for him when he came to office the next day. He opened it to find a heartfelt thank you note from Rhea. He read through it a couple of times and then typed back his response. He wanted her and everyone else in office to understand that she was given a permanent position only because she deserved it. There had been no partiality on his part. As soon as he sent the email and rested his back against the chair, his inbox pinged again. Rhea's words, 'Friends again!' filled his screen.

He smiled to himself. Before he could say yes, another e-mail came in. This time Rhea asked him to meet her at the New Moon Café the next day. *I need to talk to you*, read the e-mail.

He hesitated for a minute, his mind revolting at the

thought of agreeing to the proposal, but curiosity won him over and he replied in affirmative.

The next day after work, he combed his hair, folded his shirt's sleeves upto the elbow and walked into the coffee place, feeling both awkward and excited. Rhea was already there waiting for him, looking restlessly now and then at the main door of the cafe. He walked towards her table, gave a tentative smile and sat down next to her. Feeling that it was best to get it out of the way right at the start, he said, choosing his words carefully, "I am sorry, Rhea. I made you feel awkward. I thought you liked me too. Anyway, let's forget about it. We are better off as friends."

Rhea placed her hand softly on his knee and said, "I am sorry for breaking your heart that day. Arun, I do like you. But being a fresher, it is very embarrassing to have all the seniors gossip about me. When I saw the bouquet, the card, and all the people crowded around my desk to see what was written inside, I couldn't help myself and lashed out. I really like you."

Arun looked at her, puzzled. He had not expected this explanation at all. 'Is she just messing with me?' he wondered, but she continued, "I hope you can forgive me and we can start afresh with our relationship."

He smiled widely at her words. He had not been wrong about her feelings for him after all!

By the time they left the Café, he had forgotten all about

his embarrassment and laughed freely. He felt happiness entering back into his life. His steps began to spring again while he walked around the office.

For a while, everything seemed to have fallen into place perfectly. Sometimes, he'd catch Rhea's gaze at office and they would exchange quick smiles. She'd meet him for lunch at the cafeteria and he would often take her out for dinners. They spent a lot of time together and Arun even managed to impart to her some coding skills. He liked how things were growing between them and did not want anything to change.

One day, when Rhea called him over to help her with a new project about offline computer connections, Arun went over, happy to have the extra time to spend with her at work. They worked steadily through the evening. It was only when he finished writing the code did he realise how late it had gotten. All their colleagues had left already. The lights had been dimmed all over the floor, except for the ones over their desks. "Oh, even the guards have left," he said, turning around to face Rhea.

She tucked her hair behind her ear and smiled softly at him. Slowly, she placed her hand on the desk, leaned her body against his chair and moved closer. Arun tried to smile back, but was distracted by her face so close to his. He could feel her breath on his lips as the smell her perfume filled his nostrils.

Before she could move any closer, he forced himself to

take a deep breath and pulled away from her. He said, "Please, this is not right, especially not in the office. This is a public place. This should be a special moment and we should wait before doing anything like this."

The words tumbled out of his mouth in one breath, and he knew immediately that he had said the wrong thing.

"What…are you mad?" Asked Rhea with a furrowed brow.

When he did not reply, she continued, "I hope you are not imagining that you can only kiss in private, behind closed doors? You are such an innocent person. I have never seen boys being shy about kissing. These things are very common between people in a relationship. You are a grown man, you should know these things."

Feeling completely wrong-footed, he looked down and said, "It is just too intimate for a workplace and I feel very awkward doing it."

Rhea was silent for a few minutes. He watched her debating mentally what to do. Finally, she grabbed her purse and stood up to leave. He could do nothing to stop her, so he just walked quietly with her to the nearest bus stop. She averted her gaze away from him and left without saying a word.

That night, he tossed this way and that on his bed, unable to sleep. He did not expect to hear from her for a while, but once again an e-mail was waiting for him at office the next morning. As a final goodbye of sorts, it read:

Dear Arun,

I thought about us all through last night. We are completely different people in the way we think. I know they say opposites attract, but I don't see us going any further in this relationship. I need someone who can support me emotionally and physically. You are a marvellous person.

I just feel that my expectations and needs are different from yours. I hope you understand that we cannot continue being together anymore. I hope you find someone who understands you better.

Regards,

Rhea.

Almost mechanically, he typed a reply:

Thank you for your praises and wishes! I appreciate that you took the time to sincerely express your feelings.

Regards,

Arun

He did not mean what he said. He still did not understand what exactly had he done wrong. He sat there questioning himself, 'What is wrong with me? Why can't I connect with people like I used to before? Am I doing something wrong?' It took a few days for Arun to settle down and accept what had happened.

Chapter 4

Six months passed by unnoticed, only the pain remained in Arun's heart while he engaged himself furiously in his work. Then came the big night, the company's Achievement Awards and he bagged two titles; Up-Coming Junior and The Best Performer of the year. He was flushed with happiness. The past year had been a struggle, but he kept his head down and worked hard, and these awards served as validation for all the tiring hours that he had put in.

Grabbing a drink at the bar, he watched a short, blond haired girl in a black dress accept the award for The Most Creative Person. 'She looks pretty with those sharp facial features,' he thought idly. He knew her from around the office, but they had never really spoken to each other. Everybody seemed to be going crazy for her, as she drew the loudest cheer and applause from the crowd!

There was a certain brightness to her smile that caught his eye and he found his gaze glued to her as she moved about the room, even when Sumit stood next to him, telling him some story.

She came up to them after a while. Before she could say hello, Sumit broke off abruptly and smiled at her. "Shall I get a drink for the most deserving lady?" he asked.

Arun knew he was only trying to impress her and could not blame him for making the effort.

She nodded her head and smiled, "Thanks for the offer, Sumit."

She toyed with the hem of her dress and looked around as Sumit hurried towards the bar.

"Congratulations Arun," Adiya said softly and gave him a bright smile.

"Thank you, and congratulations to you as well! You look very good today, specially in that dress," said Arun, calmly sipping his drink.

She looked flattered and said, "Wow, thanks. Special day calls for a special dress. I'm glad you like it. I didn't think you had ever even noticed me."

He laughed at that and said, "There's nothing like that. It's just that we have never really met properly before or worked on a project together."

"So you mean to say that only the people who work together can be friends and the rest of us should never even get to know each other?" she teased him.

He was pleasantly surprised at her humour and nodded apologetically, "You've got a point there. My mistake. I will try to make friends with everyone from now on, starting with you."

This made her giggle. Adiya's presence and the sound of her laughter helped Arun relax his mind and body. She looked at the people dancing behind them and asked, "Would you like to dance?"

He hesitated for a moment; dancing was not really his forte.

She pleaded, "C'mon Arun, it will be fun!"

Just then Sumit returned with the drinks. He looked excitedly at Adiya, thrust the drinks into Arun's hands and said, "I'm ready, come. We'll dance together."

Arun was left standing there as Sumit held her hand and led her to the dance floor. Adiya looked over her shoulder at Arun with a puzzled expression. As soon as the song got over, she came back, shaking her head and making a face.

Bemused, he asked her, "Are you okay?"

She let out a loud laugh and joked, "A minute longer and I would have pretended to faint to escape from him."

He was very taken with her personality. The next day, tired but glowing from the party, he tried to focus on his work. 'Nothing is happening today,' he sighed and gave up. He headed towards the cafeteria for lunch and spotted Adiya right away, sitting in a corner by herself and eating her meal.

He went over and asked politely, "May I?"

"Yes, please! I was bored eating alone, anyway. Your company will be good," she said and gestured at him at take a chair.

"You look like you didn't get a chance to sleep properly last night," he commented, opening his stacked up steel tiffin.

She replied, "Hmm, it was almost 1 A.M. by the time I went to bed…" she trailed off, distracted by the food he had just uncovered. "What is this watery, bland looking food. It looks like hospital food. Are you on a diet? You like this food?"

He grimaced, "No, I don't like it, but I have no other option. I order from a hotel and they deliver it to the office every day. I am not lucky enough to get home cooked food like you do. I don't live with my family here." He proceeded to take a bite of his tasteless food.

"My family isn't here either, but I cook my own food every day. Eating food from outside everyday all the time is not healthy," said Adiya and pushed her tiffin towards Arun. "I am not a great cook but would you like to try some?" she offered.

He reached forward and helped himself to some curry. Flavours burst in his mouth with a single bite. Arun found it utterly refreshing over the bland food that he had been having for days. "Yummy! I am eating such good, home-cooked food after a very long time. Thank you Adiya," he exclaimed.

She smiled and offered him some more. The lunch break passed by quickly for Arun. He had a meeting scheduled after lunch, so he ate up quickly and packed his own tiffin back. Thanking Adiya, he hurried back to his desk.

Arun gathered his documents together, thinking about the lunch break, when suddenly the thought of Esha came to his mind. She too had offered him her tiffin, he remembered, that marked the beginning of their friendship.

Absentmindedly, he went for his meeting with the manager. It had been too long since Arun last thought about Esha. The manager went over the papers and summoned someone else to his cabin. Arun thoughts drifted away to how Esha must be doing in life and whether she ever thought of him too. He was pulled out of his daydream when the door opened and Adiya entered in and walked towards the manager confidently. Happily surprised, Arun looked at his manager, eager to know what lay ahead.

The manager said, "Come… sit. The client on this project wants the features to be very appealing, and fanciful. Adiya, I want you to design the screens and sit with Arun to see how they can be integrated with the code. I have given the documents containing project requirements to Arun. Go through them and discuss how to proceed amongst yourselves.

They thanked the manager and walked out of his cabin. 'We're going to be working together!' Arun thought happily. Esha's magic of sharing the tiffin seemed to hold true here as well. While walking out together, he handed over the documents to her saying, "Here, take these. I have already read them. After you're done, we can sit and decide how do go ahead with things."

She was at his desk in a couple of hours. She leaned over and placed some papers in front of him, saying, "I have created some rough sketches. Can you check if these can be incorporated into the code?"

He shuffled through the pages while she pointed out each icon and its placement. Impressed, he said, "No wonder, they gave you the most creative person award."

She laughed, "And you, Mr. Best Performer, can you put these into code?"

"I am not sure about all. Some, I can do easily, some will take time and some cannot be done at all. We will find out in a few days," said Arun, carefully considering the designs.

"Okay, you have a thorough look and let me know which ones can be incorporated and which ones cannot. Then we can discuss the same with the manager," said Adiya, shifting back and walked back towards her desk.

The manager was pleased with their plans when they went to him two days later. Adiya seemed particularly relieved and asked Arun on their way back, "How many days will it take us to finish the project, now that we have the approval?

"You seem to be in a hurry. Is the client after you to finish it quickly?" Asked Arun.

"Oh no, no," she said, "I was just hoping to be free by this weekend. A new retro pub is opening near my house and they are offering free drinks. My friends have received an invitation and they want me to join them."

He nodded understandingly, "Nice. Don't worry, I think it should get over before that."

On Friday, he walked over to her desk and told her to access the project file on her computer. She looked up with a smile and asked, "Did you upload the completed version? Let's show the manager. He should be able to access it from the network drive. Did you tell him that we are done?"

He said, "No, not yet. I thought I would show you first. The manager had asked me about it during lunch and I told him that it was almost over."

She checked it quickly for minor details. "Let's go and show it to him," she said, turning off her computer's monitor and getting up. "It looks good."

"You are always in a hurry," Arun teased, following her.

"Life is too short and I don't want to slog at office over the weekends too. Partying after work feels awesome," said Adiya and walked into the manager's office.

Later, as Arun was packing up to leave for the evening, she came up to him and asked, "Do you have any plans for the weekend? Why don't you join us?"

Arun leaned back in his chair and said, "No plans, but I won't be comfortable around new people…"

"Don't be so boring, I will be there! And it is better than wasting your weekend alone at home," she said, not giving him a chance to object. "I will see you at Café Rock at 9 P.M. on Saturday, and don't worry… you will enjoy it."

That is how, on a Saturday evening, Arun found himself outside Café Rock, taking in the sight of Adiya in a long black silk dress, waiting for him to arrive. "Here you are," she said, spotting him. She then moved closer to whisper, "Somebody is looking hot in that black shirt…I didn't know you could look so handsome. Everybody will want to be friends with you."

He felt shy and said, "Stop it. You are embarrassing me." Before he could stop himself, he added, "By the way, you look like a showstopper yourself."

That pretty smile he liked so much, flashed across her face.

Turning away, he greeted her friends and all of them

headed inside to party. He had never gone out to a place like that before. Adiya and her friends immediately got some drinks and started to dance. He tried to join in, but felt very uncomfortable. The music was too loud to engage in conversation and the dance floor was so crowded that people kept bumping into each other. A girl in a pink skirt stumbled into Arun. She turned with a smile and mouthed a sorry, before moving across the floor from where she could see him clearly while dancing. Arun gave her a short smile and turned to look at Adiya.

He was not interested in this new girl's obvious come ons. Adiya noticed the girl and said, "I told you." He just smiled and let her move closer to him. She placed a hand on his shoulder as the DJ played a romantic song. Just then, someone bumped into her from behind. He quickly put a hand around her waist to support her. She did not seem to mind and only smiled more widely. He was feeling very awkward and avoided looking at her.

He felt her hand reach around him, drawing him closer. She pulled herself to his chest and leaned forward. Her lips looked so soft to Arun from the little distance that was left between their faces. Abruptly, he jerked his head back and said, "My drink is finished. Let me get us fresh ones."

He moved quickly to the bar. When he turned around, he saw her move off the dance floor and leave the place. He ran after her, but by the time he managed to push his way through the crowd and looked down the street outside, she was gone. He had messed things up again, he realised. 'She must have gotten mad at me for rejecting her advances. But I do not want to do such things!' he thought, stressed.

Arun dragged himself home, wondering why nobody understood his emotions. He hardly understood them himself.

Arun retreated into his shell once again. In office the next day, Sumit found him eating his lunch alone after everyone else had finished. Arun did not say anything and continued munching on his bland food.

After a few moments, Sumit said, "I didn't know you were such a fool."

Taken aback, Arun raised his eyebrows at him.

"This is the second time a hot girl has approached you, and you have rejected her again," accused Sumit, looking at him curiously.

Arun did not want to engage in that conversation and snapped, "I don't like such things and I am in no mood to discuss it with you. These are personal issues."

Sumit was amused. "I hope you are not gay," he said, suppressing a smirk.

This made Arun angry and he fired back, "Not kissing someone doesn't make you gay!"

Sumit patted Arun's shoulder and said laughing, "Are you

from a different world then? Relationships without kissing don't exist these days." Composing himself soon after, he said, "Sorry, I didn't mean to offend you. I only came to offer my help. You see, I have a psychologist friend. Perhaps talking to her will help you understand why you feel this way."

Arun was still annoyed with Sumit. He packed up his tiffin and said, "I don't need to visit any psychologist to know what happened. I was just not comfortable kissing them, that's all."

Sumit said, "I know, but isn't it better to know what drove you away from kissing them? I am sure it must be bothering you too, such behaviour is quite unusual these days. What's wrong with just meeting her and having a chat? Don't worry, she is a good friend of mine. You will be fine with her."

Arun was not too keen with the idea of meeting this psychologist and just wanted to leave. However, Sumit forced a visiting card into his pocket as he stood up. "Tell her my name, when you meet her," he said. "She will sort you out."

The card sat on his desk the whole day. He was distracted and confused. Unable to take it any longer, he made a call to the number mentioned on the card and fixed an appointment before he could change his mind.

He was nervous when he walked into her office later that evening. The first thing he noticed was a board that read *"Since only the mind can be sick, only the mind can be healed. Only the mind is in need of healing."* It did nothing to calm his nerves. He took his place at the edge of a sofa and looked around at the watercolour paintings, the plants, and the decoration set against pastel walls.

He was not sure why he was there. 'Sumit thought I am gay. Did Rhea and Adiya think so too? Maybe I am gay,' he thought, his palms sweating. 'But I have felt attracted to girls before so that could not be,' he reasoned. 'It was just the wrong place at the wrong time. With Rhea, I had been at office and trying to do some work. As for Adiya, we were not even in a relationship. How could I have kissed her?'

"Hello, you must be Arun." A lady in a red and white sari appeared, interrupting his thoughts. "My name is Sima. I hope you have not been waiting long," she said.

Arun got up to shake hands with her and settled down for the session. 'She seems intelligent, perhaps she will be able to help me,' he wondered. Arun started talking and slowly all the details of his past experiences with the two women came out. He felt a little embarrassed talking to her about those things, but he knew he had to tell her everything.

She listened carefully, nodding and making notes. She considered(observed) him over the top of her notepad. "Did you feel stressed," she asked, "when you realised that they wanted to kiss you?"

He shook his head, "No, I don't think so. I just thought it was not the right time or the right place, and I didn't even know them well enough to get so intimate with them."

She started writing again. He started to feel like he was wasting his time.

She lifted her head, clapped her notebook shut and smiled at him, "What is the problem? You behaved perfectly normally. Some people just take time to feel comfortable before indulging in anything that requires commitment. You feel that in order to kiss someone, you need to be in love and committed to that person first. Everyone has the right to be different in having their own perspective of love. If perhaps you feel that you wanted to kiss them back, but your body and mind didn't permit you, then you can try the subconscious mind training technique."

He was relieved. At last, somebody could make sense of things for him. He felt glad to know that his reaction had been perfectly normal.

She continued, "See, our mind is made up of three levels; the conscious mind, the preconscious mind, and the unconscious mind. The conscious mind includes our mental processing, that of thought and speech. The preconscious mind is the ordinary mind with a capacity to pull a memory into consciousness when needed. The third level, the unconscious mind, is also called the subconscious mind. It is a reservoir of feelings, thoughts, urges, and memories that are beyond our controlled awareness."

Arun did not understand how this had anything to do with him or his situation, but she did not give him a chance to speak. She carried on, "We cannot access this information, but it is deeply engraved in our minds. Thus, despite your previous experiences, right form your childhood, being good, your deep subconscious mind could be denying you for some reason which you are not aware of."

He stared at her blankly. His mind was denying him? He didn't know what the lady was talking about. On seeing confusion rise in his eyes, she paused and said, "To find out why your mind is processing things in a particular way, I will have to hypnotise you. Till then, try meditation and visualisation. That's it for this session; that will be 2000 rupees."

Startled, he repeated, "2000 rupees?"

She said, "Yes, 2000 for now, and the rest will be calculated per session."

He thought of asking for a discount, giving the reference of Sumit, but he felt irritated enough to keep quiet.

The amount was ridiculous, but he had no choice. He walked out of the room thinking it best to just forget that the meeting ever happened. 2000 rupees just for some advice! He messaged Sumit on the way home, disgruntled that his friend had charged him with such a high fee.

Within minutes, Sumit sent a long reply:

Remember the day you and I were sitting with Rhea for lunch. How desperate she was to talk only with you, and how happy she became when I left. It hurt me. I deserved her more than you did; I trained her and she chose you over me to be her boyfriend.

Then again at the party, when Adiya danced with me, she made excuses to get away so that she could be with you. It made me look like a fool. I flirted with her, praised her, and even got a drink for her, but she only wanted to be with you.

I waited a long time to get back at you. Pain, my friend, cuts pain.

Chapter 5

Sumit's betrayal stayed with Arun for many days. It was exactly the kind of selfish games and back-stabbing he despised and had tried to distance himself from when he first started working in Mumbai. His experience made him put his guards up around his emotions, and he no longer interacted with anyone socially.

So he was surprised when he was woken up from a nap on a holiday by the shrill ring of his landline. Nobody called him at home except for his mother.

"Is this Arun Shetty?" enquired a female voice when he answered the call.

Tentatively he replied, "Yes, this is Arun. How can I help you?"

"Hello, this is Lina D'souza from St. John Missionary High

School. We are organising an alumni meet for your batch this Saturday. As an ex-student, you are invited, of course. Would you like to join us?" she asked, "I need to take a count."

He took only a moment to let the unexpected news sink in. 'How wonderful,' he thought and quickly replied, "Yes, yes, please count me in. I will definitely be there."

She laughed at his excited tone, and said "I'm glad you can make it. We have arranged for a bus facility as several points, would you like to opt in for that as well?"

"Oh, great! I will take the bus," he said, hit with the nostalgia of his school bus days. "Do you know anyone else who is taking the bus?" he asked.

She said, "I can't be certain, but many have requested for it. I am sure you will meet a lot of your friends on the bus."

They discussed the details and Arun put down the receiver of his landline with a click, feeling happier than he had in weeks. A boyish smile played on his lips just at the thought of his school days in Mumbai. After eight long years, he finally had the opportunity to meet everybody again. He could already feel the exhilaration setting in.

The next four days flew by in a haze of anticipation. On Saturday, he reached the assigned bus stop well in time. He was dressed in a white shirt and blue jeans. The scorching sun above his head was making him perspire. He stood fidgeting with his watch and looked around, trying to catch a familiar face from among the people milling about.

Someone tapped his shoulder, "Arun? Is that you?"

He turned around eagerly. It was Rohit! "Rohit, my friend, how are you? You look just the same! Except for the overgrown beard on your face, of course!" he exclaimed, pulling him into a hug.

Some other people started to recognise him and came over to say hello. The air buzzed with laughter and excited greetings. Arun's friends taunted him, "You look so smart, how many girlfriends do you have?" and he laughed it off, for once not minding all the gossip.

Much to his amusement, all his school friends looked very different from how he remembered them. Some of them had put on weight while some had become thin, some wore spectacles and some had grown very attractive.

Among all these people, Arun's eyes were searching for Esha, but she was nowhere to be seen. When the bus bearing their school name arrived and everybody started to board, he gave up looking for her, disappointed. Just then, a girl drove up to them on a bike. 'Esha?' he thought, with a glimmer of hope. But it was not her. Priyanka took off her helmet and waved at the boys. He set his hopes aside and went over to say hello. Joining in the teasing with others, he said, "Oh my God, Priyanka! You still haven't left the habit of reaching late all the time."

Joking around, they got onto the bus together, automatically heading towards the last row of seats. As the conductor was about to close the gates shut, a girl climbed aboard. She wore a blue dress and her long hair were hanging down her back. 'There she is,' he smiled and watched Esha walk cautiously towards him.

"What is this?" she complained, pretending to be upset, "I used to keep a seat for everyone and no one has kept one for me."

Arun jumped up immediately and offered her his seat. "For you, your highness," he said.

Everybody laughed and Esha smiled at him sweetly. "Thank you Arun," she said, taking the seat. He noticed how quaintly she sat down, careful of her dress and hair. He hardly recognised her from the short haired, messy girl she used to be.

Rohit seemed to have made the same observation. He said, "Arun, isn't Esha looking very different? You remember how she used to be in school. The Esha we knew would not be caught dead in a dress like that or wearing such fancy jewellery." Turning to Esha, he continued, "Who are you and what have you done to the real Esha?"

Esha grinned at Rohit's remark and mock punched his shoulder, making him laugh even more.

Arun stood beside them, amusedly observing every move of hers, the way she laughed, talked, teased and made faces. He could not take his eyes off of her. Through the years, he had always wondered what she must look like, and at that moment, there she was in front of him, absolutely dazzling.

Suddenly, the bus jerked forward to start and he grabbed the rod over the seat to maintain his balance. His hand landed on Esha's and for one moment he felt the warmth of her skin under his palm. She quickly slipped her hands away from under his and placed them in her lap. She avoided his eye and turned to speak with the others. Feeling awkward, he moved back and held the top bar for the rest of the journey.

The school had not changed in the least. He felt a fond rush of memories when he first caught sight of the building and the grounds, thronging with students. It was a pure moment of joy and he felt as if they were still studying in school. There was excitement and glee in each person's eyes. The gathering hall turned chaotic with all the ex-students talking among themselves, catching up on each other's lives.

"Welcome students, we meet again after so many years," boomed the voice of his favourite teacher, Ms. Grace Luis.

He cheered with everybody, overwhelmed with excitement. The teacher then instructed them to move to their old classrooms. Chattering and reminiscing about all the games they used to play as kids, he walked through the colorfully sketched corridors with his friends. His classroom felt smaller than he remembered, or perhaps he felt himself too big for the room. Without realising it, they all formed into their old groups.

Arun sat down in the exact row he used to sit in with

Esha and waited for her to come sit next to him. But before she came in, Rohit claimed her seat. Slightly disappointed, he kept quiet and watched her take the seat in front of them with Priyanka. He wanted to speak to her and know how she had been all this while, but she was too busy talking to everyone else. He only managed to exchange a couple of short sentences directed towards him.

Mr Jackson, their old class teacher, walked into the room carrying a book. Arun turned away to stand up with everyone else to wish him.

"How are you all, my children?" he smiled at them, "Every one of you is now a different shape and size, but I bet you all are still as naughty as before!"

The class echoed with laughter. Some people crowded around him, making him remember stories about all the trouble they use to cause as his students. Some were married, some even had kids, some were working in high-profile jobs; each one of them had a story to tell. Arun wanted to know Esha's story, but it looked like she was not interested in him at all.

His smile faltered a little at the thought. Just then, she turned to him and said, "Hey, give me your number. I don't even have it anymore."

Annoyed, he snapped at her, "Why do you need my number? You've spent all of tonight behaving as if I am a stranger."

He regretted saying it immediately, but Esha only looked at him with a blank expression.

"Okay, don't give it then," she said, unbothered.

She resumed her conversation with everyone else, leaving him to sit and brood over her strange behaviour. Where had their special connection gone? He felt as though all the friendship that they had shared meant nothing to her anymore.

A bitter sweet feeling swept through him as he said goodnight to everyone later. Such a beautiful night, slightly marred by his encounter with Esha. It stayed on his mind all through work over the next week.

Rohit called him the next weekend to chat, happy to have reconnected with him after so many years. They caught up on each other's lives and what all they were up to those days. Arun lazed on his bed, waves of nostalgia hitting him again as they spoke about their school days when they shared everything, be it their tiffins, holiday homework, or a game of cricket under the old banyan tree.

"It is good that we finally managed to get in touch. All thanks to Esha for organising the alumni meet. Such a great idea," said Rohit, jolting Arun out of his day dream. Arun sat up straight and paid attention.

Oblivious to the fact that he had just delivered the most surprising information for Arun, Rohit continued, "She went to the school and spoke to them about arranging everything.

You have no idea how she went out of the way to make them find your whereabouts in Nagpur and track you down from there."

'It was Esha behind this whole reunion!' Arun felt remorseful for how he had been so short with her. "Are you serious?" he asked, trying to make sense of Rohit's words. "She barely even spoke to me the whole evening. I thought she must have forgotten all about me."

Rohit simply laughed at his confusion and said, "She is angry with you. After you left Mumbai, you never kept in touch. She waited for you to write and you never did. She was very eager to meet you after so long, but you know her, she doesn't express these feelings easily."

Feeling relieved, Arun stood up from his bed in excitement. 'It was all just a big misunderstanding,' he thought. He had to speak to her immediately. "Give me her number, Rohit. I'll talk to her right away."

Impatiently, Arun dialed her number and waited for her to pick up the phone. 'There is so much to talk about!' he thought.

"Hello?" Esha's sweet voice filtered into his ear.

"So," he started, "You are angry with me?"

"Arun! How did you get my number?" she sounded utterly surprised to hear from him. "Of course, I am angry with you. I never heard from you all these years. You left

Mumbai and just disappeared. That was it."

Feeling a little guilty, he replied quickly, "I did send you a couple of emails, but you never wrote back! I thought you must have gotten busy with studies and did not have time for me so I didn't try anymore."

"Oh Arun!" she said, "that email ID from school? You know how we were, I hardly ever checked it. And then I forgot the password and just created a new one. I should have written to you."

"Yeah, you should have sent a letter or called me." he added. "Why didn't you call me? I gave you the house number before I left."

His words seemed to make Esha sad. She remained silent for a few seconds and then said, "I thought since you had moved to a new school, you wouldn't want me pushing you to be my friend anymore. I thought, perhaps it would be best for me to just wait for you to tell me that you missed me, but I didn't get any of your letters, and then it just got too late to call you. Too much time had passed."

He felt his heart aching over their missed connection and all the time that they had lost due to the misunderstanding. He said, "Ah Esha! How could you ever imagine that I would stop caring about our friendship? We were best friends, of course I missed you. I thought about you so often."

His voice tightened with emotion, "But you know, it's all in the past now, and here we are. Let's make the most of it."

He knew she too must be feeling as bad as he was and tried to lighten the mood. “So now you’ll have to meet me and apologize in person,” he quipped lightly.

“Sure… let’s meet at Uncle’s shop tomorrow at 4 P.M.,” she said with a smile in her voice. “Bye Arun, I’m glad you called me.”

A strong whiff of coffee and cakes greeted him as he walked into Uncle’s shop the next day. He breathed in the familiar aroma and took in the ambience of his old hangout. Not a lot had changed at that place, he noted, only the regular fixtures in places. He couldn’t believe he was back there with Esha again.

He spotted her, sitting and observing closely the people passing by the cash counter.

He sat down next to her and smiled, “I always found you fascinated by the counter whenever we used to come here. Tell me, what is so interesting about it?”

Esha fiddled with the sleeve of her red top and said, “It is uncle himself who I find so interesting; the way he asks after each person and whether they liked their coffee or not. With the regulars, he always makes sure to ask about their families, work and such things. To see him maintain such a relationship with his customers, it is something really special. He seems genuinely happy serving people.”

Arun turned around to look at uncle, a white-haired man, probably in his sixties, greeting every person who walked past his counter with a bright smile. He had never noticed him from Esha's perspective before.

She took a sip of her coffee and continued, "Do you know, out of each earning he makes, he puts one rupee aside in a separate box. I asked him about it once and he told me it was for the boys who work here. At the end of every month, they get this extra money to spend it over whichever delicacy they like. Isn't that beautiful? Hearing about small things like this gives me a sense of real happiness."

They were interrupted by the waiter asking for their order.

"I'll have a coffee too. Oh! do you still make those small sweet cakes?" he asked.

"Yes we do," the waiter replied, "Shall I get you one?"

He looked at Esha enquiringly and said, "Actually, get us two of those."

She smiled and said, "You used to love them. I remember you would have one each time we came here, savouring every last crumb."

"I miss the taste. I have tried those cakes at so many places, but the softness and the richness of chocolate that they have in their cakes here is incomparable," he reminisced. "I remember how you loved the masala buns from that other place. How many times we've missed the bus to go eat them!"

"Hmm, my favourite," she said, "and remember, how

Rohit used to cry all the time that we never took him to eat the buns with us?"

"You don't take me anywhere," Arun mockingly imitated him.

Esha's eyes crinkled with amusement at all the funny little stories they remembered from their school days. He soon realised that beneath all that smart dressing and beautiful hair, his Esha was still the same; sweet and naughty at the same time. He did not feel the time fly by as they talked and laughed into the evening, over repeated orders of sweet cakes and coffee.

He didn't want to leave, but eventually Esha looked at her watch and exclaimed, "It is already past 7! We've been here for hours. We'd better leave."

They left the shop together and walked slowly to the bus stop. He couldn't help but desire to spend more time together with her. "What are you doing next weekend? Are you free?" he stopped her and asked. "I'll be free from work then and I was wondering if we could plan a get together with everyone. Maybe go to the beach or something?"

She seemed excited at the suggestion. She nodded and said, "Yes, that's a great idea! Let's plan this with Rohit and Priyanka. It'll be so much fun to spend a weekend together again."

Chapter 6

They ended up planning a whole road-trip to Alibaug for the weekend. The weather was nice and everyone agreed that a bike ride would be fun. Rohit and Arun were the first to arrive at the meeting spot. Leaning against their bikes they waited for the others to arrive. Priyanka reached soon after, followed by two other friends of theirs, Puja and Prakash.

Arun checked his watch over and over again. Esha was the only one who hadn't arrive yet. It was not like her to be late, he thought, looking down the street, not paying attention to the Royal Enfield Thunderbird that came to a halt just beside them. The rider turned off the powerful engine and he heard her sweet voice float towards him, "Who are you waiting for? We are all here now."

He turned to look and gasped at the sight of Esha, comfortably sitting astride the metallic bike, looking cool in a pair of blue jeans and a simple white T-shirt. She took off her helmet and shook her long hair loose.

"Are you going to ride that bike all the way to Alibaug?" he heard Rohit ask.

"Of course. You said we were taking bikes for this trip," she said calmly, "Priyanka can come along with me."

Recovering from his amazement, Arun cut her off saying, "Priyanka is riding with Rohit. We thought we'd take just three bikes between the six of us so we can all ride with each other. You can sit with me, if you'd like."

Esha was undeterred and said immediately, "That's not a problem. We'll take my bike as the third one. You can sit behind me."

He was taken aback. How could he sit behind a girl and let her ride? But there was no arguing with Esha's challenging gaze. He looked at Rohit helplessly, only to be told to sit with Esha and stop wasting time.

Left with no choice, he deposited his bike at a friendly shop-owner's place and moved to sit behind Esha. The other boys sniggered while starting their bikes and all of them rode off. He adjusted himself on the seat behind Esha as she put on her helmet. The bike started with a thunderous growl and with a brief screeching of tires, they too were off.

He couldn't help but fear that Esha would not be able to balance the bike well or know how to ride properly. He kept his eyes on the road, making her aware of every speed breaker and car passing by. Esha, however, didn't seem to be listening to him at all.

He balanced himself with much difficulty. He even found himself bumping into Esha a few times when she applied brakes. To support himself, he held onto the back rest tightly, but it soon grew inconvenient for him. After a while, he left the backrest, too distracted by the scene around to be bothered about falling anymore.

From stray animals and people crossing the road to the other vehicles speeding past, Esha manoeuvred her way through the Mumbai traffic with ease. She kept up a smooth, steady pace and he slowly started to relax. She was clearly a skilled rider and despite himself, Arun was impressed.

"When did you learn to ride a bike so well?" he leaned forward and yelled over the wind.

"A long time back, almost six years ago. My cousin taught me after I bugged him for ages," she shouted back.

"I have never even sat behind a girl who rides a bike, let alone this well," he said, "but I feel completely relaxed with you."

"That's pretty weird," she said. "A lot of my female friends ride the bike and I can assuredly say that we are no less than boys at it. And please, girls can even fly a plane today, riding a bike is nothing compared to that."

He laughed, "It's true, girls can do anything. You've made me realise this today."

He sat back relaxed, allowing the wind to caress his face and soothe him. They had left the city limits behind and Arun realised that it had been a while since he enjoyed such scenic beauty. Everything felt simple and magical; the sunlight filtering down on them through the trees, the open fields, the smell of the sea in the air, and the birds floating lazily in the sky. It lulled him into a haze, and he didn't notice when he leaned his head against Esha's back and dozed off.

He was jerked awake when the bike halted abruptly. Disoriented, he rubbed his eyes and said, "What… Have we reached already?"

"No no, not yet," Esha shook her head, "you fell asleep against me and I was having troubling balancing like that, so I stopped here."

He yawned and said, "Sorry about that. It felt too nice sitting behind you and riding so smoothly. I couldn't help but fall asleep."

She smiled, "That's okay. Good to know that you are so comfortable back there. Shall we go ahead or do you want to stop here for some time?"

He took a water bottle out of his bag and sprinkled some water on his face. "Let's go ahead, the others will wonder where we went."

"Are you sure? I'll have to tie you to me to stop you from falling," she joked.

He laughed at the prospect. "Come now, you've covered most of the distance. Let me ride the bike for a while. You can sit behind me and enjoy the scenery."

This time, Esha conceded and happily switched places with Arun.

He started the bike and they were off again, whizzing down the winding road. It was almost afternoon when they reached Alibaug, coming to a stop in front of a beautiful white villa surrounded by coconut trees. The others had already parked and were waiting for them in the garden.

"Wow, Rohit. Good choice booking this villa, it looks amazing!" Esha said appreciatively, walking through the tall entrance gates.

Parking the bike next to the others, Arun found himself pleasantly surprised at all the greenery around. The shrubs along the path were carefully tended and flowers were in full bloom everywhere. He listened carefully and realised that the dull roar in the air was the sound of waves crashing nearby. After the madness of city life, this was exactly the kind of peace and quiet he needed.

He followed the others into the house and heard Esha call out, "Let's freshen up first guys, then we can explore the place."

Inside, they were met by an old caretaker, a palm tree printed shirt hanging loosely off his frame. He bowed his head in welcome and said, "Come in, I had just gone around the back to check the water supply. I hope you did not have any trouble finding the place."

Rohit moved forward to shake hands with him, "No trouble at all. We thought we'll just settle in first. Can you show us the rooms?"

"Yes, of course. Please follow me," he gestured down the hallway.

The rooms were big and airy, decorated with paintings of tribal women here and there. Arun sat down on the edge of the bed and stretched, tired from the long ride. They took turns taking quick showers and getting ready. The caretaker had promised them hot lunch and the aroma of the food cooking made Arun's stomach grumbled with hunger.

"This is a feast! It has been ages since I last had such delicious food," he groaned in delight half an hour later, biting into a particularly juicy piece of garlic chicken.

Everybody nodded, too busy eating to respond.

After a while, Esha said, "This is as good as your mother's cooking, Arun. Remember that sweet vegetable rice you used to get in your tiffin for lunch? It used to be my favourite."

He swallowed a bit and said, "In that case, you will soon

get to eat it again. She is coming to Mumbai next week to get her knees examined."

"What happened to her knees?" enquired Esha, concern colouring her voice.

"She is unable to walk properly because her knees ache badly all the time," he said, taking another piece of chicken.

"Which doctor are you planning to consult?" she asked, finishing her food and sitting back.

"We haven't decided yet. I've been asking around but we haven't zeroed in on one still," he said, wiping his hands with a tissue.

Rohit spoke up from the other end of the table, "Why don't you take her to Esha's father? He is a renowned orthopaedic doctor."

"Yes," Esha agreed immediately. "I was just about to say that. I will have a word with Dad and let him know about aunty. You just bring her to his clinic."

Arun looked up and smiled. He felt good to be around his real friends again. He trusted these people, and he knew they would never play with his emotions and his life like the people at his workplace had.

"Come on Arun," Prakash called out, "let's have a game of cricket for old times' sake."

After finishing their food, everyone headed out. Puja asked Esha to teach her how to ride the bike, while the rest tired themselves out playing cricket. Priyanka strolled around in the garden area, talking to someone on the phone.

The sun had set, but its bright orange colour still lingered in the sky when they trooped back into the house.

Later at night, Arun sat with his friends, completely content and at peace with himself, when somebody suggested that they should all go to the beach. It sounded like the most pleasant end to a perfect day.

He could see that the girls looked uneasy at the idea of venturing out into the dark narrow lane leading to the beach, but not wanting to stay at the house by themselves, they came along anyway. They had not reached far when the lack of street lights and ominous looking shadows of the trees got too much for Esha to take. She clawed the back of his jacket and whispered, "Please let's go back. It's so dark and scary here."

The two of them told the others to go ahead and returned to the house themselves. Once back, they sat in the garden, discussing how nice it was to get away from the city and enjoy each other's company like that again.

Esha folded her legs to sit comfortably, loosened her long hair and said, "I never even asked you what work you do, Arun. Tell me about it."

He took a moment to scratch his arm where the mosquitoes had started to bite him before replying, "I am working as a software engineer, but I also deal with a lot of hardware related work. What about you, what is your field of work?"

"I work at an interior design company. It's so interesting, I get to design people's dream houses," she said, smiling.

Esha gave a sudden scream and fell out of her chair. Arun looked up startled, but it was only Rohit who had creeped up on her from behind. He burst out laughing, teasing Esha for getting freaked out so easily. She sat there quietly, listening to everyone call her out for getting scared of little things. Arun noted the annoyed expression on her face.

She tied her hair back up, wore her slippers and stood up. "Arun, are you coming for a walk on the beach or not?"

Without waiting for his reply, she turned around and walked rapidly out of the gate and towards the beach. He jumped up and followed her immediately.

"Are you sure you want to go now?" he asked, catching up with her, "we can go in the morning."

She looked back towards the villa and hc could tell how angry and upset she was at being teased. "Yes, we are going now," she said and continued. He fell in step with her and they walked on in silence for a bit.

It was a full moon night, and the glimmering moon-light danced across the surface of water in mesmerising patterns. The sea felt calming, with its waves crashing ceaselessly against the shore. He felt Esha relax beside him, all that anger dissipating in the face of such a beautiful night.

"I like the love that the sea and the seashore share," she said softly.

Confused, he asked, "Love between the sea and the seashore? What is that?"

She smiled inwardly and said, "The mighty sea travels with his companions; boats, sailors and the sea creatures together they visit many destinations. When he gets tired from all his travels, he comes to the seashore and crashes down onto her, surrendering everything that he has. The seashore keeps her arms wide open when he reaches for her, to soothe his tired body and take away his pain. The moment he is relieved of his pain, he longs to go back, and the seashore lets him go."

"So, the seashore is always the sacrificing one in this love story?" he asked, thinking it over deeply.

She bent down to pick up a shell. Turning it over in her hands, she said, "No. The seashore lets him go as she knows that love is not about binding someone to yourself. To love is to let go. If they really love you, they will come back to you."

She walked up to the edge of the sea and Arun watched her splash some water around with her feet. He stood at a distance, letting her words sink in. She had all these amazing thoughts, he realized, there was still so much left to know about her. Esha giggled at the seriousness of his expression, and splashed some sea water at his face without warning him. Spluttering in shock, he tried to chase her. Her laughter rang out loud across the shore and he stopped with a smile, watching her play around with joy. Never before had he felt so good and peaceful in his life.

That night he fell asleep thinking about the sea and the seashore and the love they shared. He woke up refreshed and made his way out to the garden. He found Esha sitting there, sipping on a cup of coffee, while a white puppy played around her feet. She patted its head gently and picked it up in her arms.

Considering the prospect of an early morning walk on the beach, he headed towards the gate. He soon heard Esha call out, "Are you going to the beach?"

He paused and turned to look at her, "Yes, do you want to come along?"

She walked towards him, circling the rim of her coffee cup with a finger.

She looked preoccupied and lost, he observed. "Thinking about something?" he asked lightly. "Nothing much," she shrugged, "just how life will change after marriage."

"Marriage…?" He was stunned, nobody had mentioned anything about getting married till now. "Are you getting married?" he asked in disbelief.

"Not right away, but my parents are searching for a well-established Roman Catholic boy for me. They want me to get married soon," she replied, sounding a little distant.

He could hardly digest the news and asked, "So you will marry according to your parent's wishes?"

She gave him a wry smile. "I don't have a choice. My parents are strictly against love marriage. Even if I find someone suitable, he must belong to a certain religion, status and background."

"The girl who talks so deeply about love is going in for an arranged marriage?" He looked at her, trying to understand what was going through her mind.

Esha looked away. Twirling a strand of her hair around a finger, she said, "Love can happen anytime. Perhaps I will fall in love with the boy I get married to."

"Yes, that is always possible," he said, giving her a confused smile.

Chapter 7

The next week, Arun was asked to fly to Dubai on short notice for a new work project. It was bad timing all around. His mother was supposed to be coming to Mumbai for her treatment, which had to be postponed till he got back. It was only supposed to be a two-week trip initially, but right when he was preparing to return, he was informed that his stay had been extended by a month or so more. Arun felt helpless. On one hand he didn't want his mother to suffer her knee-pain anymore, while on the other, he couldn't refuse the opportunity of the first official trip to a foreign country. Even though he was ready to drop his official trip for the sake of his mother, he was not allowed to do so by his seniors at work. The regret of not being able to help his mother kept pricking him throughout, souring the excitement he anticipated in coming to Dubai.

Giving up the hope of returning any time soon, he spoke to his parents, "No Dad, they won't let me come back in between. Listen, I have spoken to Esha's father and have confirmed the appointment. You and Ma can head to Mumbai immediately, all the necessary arrangements are taken care of, don't worry."

He felt that he was letting his parents down, but he had no choice. He decided to call Esha to let her know as well. He was sure she would help him. Just as he had expected, she was understanding as ever and assured him that she would handle things for him back in Mumbai. Esha visited his parents as soon as they reached the city and arranged for their trip to her father's clinic. When her father recommended a knee replacement surgery, she took a couple of days off from work to take care of Arun's mother. She made arrangements for their stay at the clinic and instructed the staff there to make the best provisions for Arun's mother.

Once she was back on her feet, she called Arun to tell him everything that Esha had done for her. With immense gratitude, she said, "Arun, she is a beautiful girl. She has shown me such love and support, we never lacked in anything. I feel very thankful to her for everything she did for us."

He listened smiling, touched by the depth of Esha's kindness. He dialed her immediately after and said, "Thank you, Esha. Thank you for all your effort in looking after my mother. She adores you."

"It was my duty to look after my best friend's mother in his absence. There is no need of thanks," she said simply.

Arun was amazed by the ease with which she justified all that she did in such a simple manner. That girl always surprised him with her outlook on life.

He told his mother the same thing the next time he spoke to her, a week later.

He could hear the smile in her voice as she said, "You are lucky to have her as your friend."

She paused for a moment and then continued, "Esha called me on Thursday and invited me to her engagement party. Her grandmother is not keeping well, so her family wants to get her married off soon."

A sudden wave of sadness hit him. Everything was happening so quickly, while he was stuck in Dubai, unable to be there for such an important event in Esha's life. He asked, "Will you and Dad attend it? I'm sure she will appreciate your presence. I don't think I will be back in time for it."

"Yes, we already have made plans to go. Although, is everything okay? She didn't sound very happy when I spoke to her," his mother asked concerned.

"Actually, she hasn't even spoken to me about her engagement. Perhaps she is tense because her parents are rushing things," he mused aloud, "I will speak to her and find out what's bothering her."

"Okay, Arun. I'll hang up now. Take care of yourself and eat your food on time," she said, saying goodbye.

He took a moment to think about what he was going to say, then slowly dialed Esha's number. He could feel the sadness in her tone as soon as she said hello.

"Congratulations Esha," he said, "Ma told me about your engagement. It was sweet of you to call my parents. I am sorry I will not be able to make it there myself."

"Thank you. Everything is happened so quickly that I got no time to let you know of it. Your mother must have told you, my Granny is not keeping well and everybody in the family wants to see me settled before anything happens to her."

Wanting to show his support, he said, "I understand how these things get. Don't worry, it will all work out, and I'll be there soon to help with everything. Now tell me, who is the lucky guy?"

"His name is George," she cleared her throat and said, "he is a Roman Catholic boy and works at Dad's clinic. When George's father offered the marriage proposal, Dad couldn't say no."

He listened carefully as she described her to-be-husband and the plans for their wedding, wondering what all he had missed out on by being in Dubai. He couldn't wait to get back to Mumbai and meet him in person. On the day of the engagement, Rohit sent him photos of the couple from the ceremony. Esha looked beautiful in a long red dress, her hair falling in curls down her back. In the photos, she had a wide smile on her face and she looked pleased to be standing next to George.

He sat looking at the pictures late into the night. He was happy for her, but sad for their friendship at the same time. 'She won't have as much time to spend with me now,' he thought. 'Things change after marriage and our bond might not survive her new changed life.'

Nostalgia for the old days stayed with him till he got back to Mumbai. On the first weekend he got, he made his way to her house, eager to meet her after so long. He was struck by her radiant beauty and glowing skin when she opened the door. Being engaged suited her well.

"You are finally here! Come, you must meet Granny, I've told her so much about you," she said, tugging him inside.

Walking through the hallway, they headed towards a room on the right. On entering, he saw a frail old woman, in a cotton sari was lying in a bed by the window.

"Granny, my best friend has come to meet you," Esha said, helping her sit up and put on her spectacles.

Granny peered at him and asked, "Oh, is that Arun?"

"Yes, he couldn't come for the engagement so he has come today, specially to meet us," Esha said happily.

He touched Granny's feet and said hello.

Granny smiled sweetly at him. Esha leaned closer to

Granny and said, "Isn't she beautiful?"

He smiled as Granny patted Esha's hand and said, "This girl is always talking about you. She is everything I have. I just want her to be happy."

He noticed how Esha looked at her. Her eyes were full of love and affection for the old lady and the bond they shared between them was almost palpable .

Someone called out Esha's name from outside just then. She got up, gesturing to Arun to follow her. "Let's go. Dad is here, we will meet him."

Arun remembered Esha's father from his school days; always very proper and strict. He hadn't changed one bit, he realized. They had a short chat about his work and his mother's health before he was summoned to check on a patient.

Esha chattered away for a while, talking about George and their plans for a life together. Before either one realized, it was time to say goodbye.

"I'm sorry, I cannot stay longer," he said to her, "I need to go home and get things in order. Shall I meet Granny now and tell her I will come again?"

She nodded, "No problem. Of course, I understand you must have so many things to do."

They went back to Granny's room where she was sipping on a hot cup of tea. Arun walked upto her and bent down to say goodbye. Granny took his hand in hers and said, "Please take care of my granddaughter. She is a very special and emotional girl. It is my last wish that you always love her and keep her happy."

Arun was baffled to see Granny's eyes swimming with tears. He wiped them away gently and turned back to look at Esha, unable to understand what she meant.

"Oh Granny," Esha said, sitting down next to her and stroking her back, "I think you got things mixed up. This is not my fiancé…this is Arun, Granny."

Granny squinted in confusion and reached for her spectacles. "I couldn't see properly without these…Arun, I know you are her best friend. Promise me you will take care of her when I am gone."

Arun sat down on her other side and consoled her, "Don't worry, Granny. I will take care of her. And where are you going, by the way? You have to be with us. We need you!"

He turned to smile at Esha and she looked back at him with warmth and respect.

That moment brimming with emotion stayed with him for many days thereafter.

The next time he saw Esha was at a party at Rohit's house, an informal celebration of her engagement. He had invited all their friends, and everybody was looking forward to meet and know George. However, Esha arrived alone. Arun heard her explaining to Rohit how George had some important appointment at the clinic and could not come.

He noticed however, that despite not turning up for the party due to the important appointment, George kept calling Esha on her phone throughout the night.

At one point, Rohit and Arun were discussing who had been the most notorious person in their class. Arun pointed towards Rohit straight away, but Rohit shook his head and insisted that it was Esha. They turned towards her, but she gestured at them to wait a minute as she was on call. One minute turned to fifteen before she finally came over. "Yes, tell me?" she said, phone still in her hand.

"Nothing, we were just debating who was more notorious in our class; you or Rohit," he said. "He thinks it was you, for sure."

She laughed and was about to say something when her phone started ringing again. Making an apologetic face, she moved away to answer the call.

Arun's lips pursed in annoyance at her behaviour. It wasn't very nice of her to come to a party thrown for her by her very own friends, just to spend all her time stuck to the phone,' he thought to himself.

Rohit must have read his expression as he defended her, saying, "This happens in all new relationships. Just give her some time to find a balance."

Priyanka called him away to enquire where the drinks were kept. Rohit gave Arun's shoulder a pat before going to help her.

His words made Arun acknowledge the loneliness in his own life. He stood alone on the terrace, a beer in hand, contemplating his life when Esha walked up to him. He looked at her as she put her phone in her purse and smiled at him. 'She always looks so effortlessly good, even in a simple white dress that she has on tonight,' he couldn't help but think.

"Lost in thought?" Esha waved her hand in front of his face.

He regained his composure, still a little annoyed with her for having been on her phone for most of that evening. "It's nothing," he said, taking a sip of his beer. "Just thinking about things. Life is strange sometimes, don't you think?"

Esha placed a hand on his shoulder and said, "I have never seen you like this before, Arun. What is bothering you so much?"

Her concern tore down his walls. He looked at her sadly and spilled his heart out. He said, "I am tired of being alone. Not that my parents are not there for me, but the thought of my future makes me sad. Once you go away too, I will be all the more alone. I just need a simple girl who understands me and is capable of being my best friend. Someone I can share everything about my life with."

Pensively, she responded, "God has made someone special for everyone; when your time comes, you will definitely meet her. Besides, I am not going anywhere...I will always be there for you." She then added, "I am your best friend, Arun. You can't let anyone else share this status with me."

He was surprised at the hurt in her voice at those last words. Arun turned her face towards himself and pulled her into a tight hug. "I will only ever have one best friend in my life and it'll be you, I promise. Now smile, my cutie pie."

He said it without a moment's thought. He had never used such words for anyone before, but Esha seemed happy to hear it. It had rolled off his tongue so spontaneously, that he was surprised at himself. Later that night, he justified it by convincing himself that it was only meant as a term of endearment for someone so special to him.

There was no time to ponder over such emotions, however. Esha's wedding was a little over a month away and a lot of shopping had to be done. Most evenings after work, he accompanied her, appreciating her all the more every day for the love and care she showed while buying gifts for everybody. He often wondered whether George noticed these little things in her, the love and care that coloured all her actions.

George never went shopping with them, and the first time Arun met him was at Priyanka's birthday party. It became immediately clear to Arun and his friends that he was not enjoying himself much. He stayed aloof and hardly spoke to anyone. He didn't even allow Esha to spend a lot of time with her friends, complaining how bored he was without her constant attention towards him.

Arun was standing by himself in a corner, observing Esha, when Rohit came over, handed him a beer and said, "Love is a strange game, isn't it? Look what a change has come about in Esha ever since her marriage got fixed. Friends have taken a back seat for her."

He looked in Esha's direction and nodded his head in agreement. She was standing next to George and talking to him. As she tried to excuse herself to go somewhere, George gestured at her to stop and led her away with him.

George's possessive nature made Arun very unhappy. His worst fears were realised when he called Esha the next day to talk about some shopping plans and she refused.

Instead, she suggested in a low voice, "Shall we go to uncle's shop today?"

The minute he saw her there, he knew something was wrong. Esha was not her usual self. She sat at the table, fidgeting with her coffee mug, clearly tensed and agitated about something.

He kept trying to make her reveal what was wrong, but she deflected all his questions and avoided talking too much. Every time it felt like he was getting somewhere, they were interrupted by a call or a message from George. Finally, she told George on the call that she was busy shopping and would talk to him later, and put her phone away.

Puzzled, Arun asked her, "Why did you hide the fact that

you are with me?"

"He is very possessive. He thinks that since I am always hanging around with you, I might fall in love with you. I have tried reasoning with him so many times, but he doesn't listen," said Esha, banging her mug down on the table.

"Yes," he replied gravely, "I figured this was the case at Priyanka's party that he did not like you talking to other people."

He had to know what she thought about it and leaned forward to ask her directly, "How will you ever meet me once you are married? He has a problem with us being friends. You can't lie to him all the time."

Esha did not say anything, and he looked at her stupefied, silently urging her to say something.

"So, you will choose to let go of our friendship for him?" he sneered, hurt by her silence. "Okay then, I should go. Love has always outdone friendship anyway."

She buried her face in her hands, unable to look at him. Shaking with disbelief, he called out to the waiter for the bill and stood up to leave.

Esha started sobbing and finally turned her head up to look at him. Seeing her so distraught, he couldn't contain himself and broke down too. Sitting down again, he held her hands and said, "I am always there for you, Esha. You are my best friend. I can never forget you. I hope that George understands our friendship someday. Till then, I think it will be best that we do not meet. Otherwise, it will ruin your relationship with him. I understand your situation...but you are so special to me that the thought of leaving you breaks my heart. I will miss you."

She wiped her tears and said softly, "I will miss you too, Arun. To start a new relationship, I am forced to end my friendship with you. It is wrong, but I have no choice. I am helpless for the sake of my family's happiness."

He returned home that night with his feeling of loneliness magnified. He had said his final farewell to Esha, knowing that they would not speak again. Deep down he knew that it was necessary for their friendship to be sacrificed, for her to have a happy relationship with her husband in future, but it did not help one bit to ease his pain.

Chapter 8

To his surprise, Arun received a call from Esha only a few days later.

"George has organised a party at my house for all my friends. He is sorry to have kept me away from everyone and would really like to get to know all of you this time. He understands our friendship and wants you to be there as well," she hurriedly explained on the phone.

He was sceptical about the invitation initially, but Rohit convinced him to go. When Arun got there, Esha seemed ecstatic to see him. Feeling relieved that everything was normal again, he went up to her and asked, "How is Granny doing?"

"Would you like to meet her?" She smiled and led him to her room.

Inside, George was sitting beside Granny, talking on the phone. He smiled when they entered and gesturing that he would be back in a minute, he left the room.

Arun nodded back at him before drawing close to Granny to say hello. She placed her wrinkled hands on his head and said, “You both look great together. I am very happy for you. You know, Esha’s grandfather and I were also deeply in love, just like the two of you are.”

Arun jumped as a loud crash interrupted Granny. It was George, standing in the doorway with an ugly expression on his face. He had just dropped his phone, astounded by Granny’s words.

“Granny, where are your spectacles?” Esha said, trying to fill the ensuing silence. “You have gotten confused again. This is my friend Arun, remember?”

Going over to George, she said, “And this is my fiancé.” She held George’s arm and tugged at his hand, drawing him inside the room. But George had turned red with anger. He pushed Esha’s hands away and stormed out of the room. Esha stumbled and followed after him, calling out to him to come back.

Disturbed by the sudden change of events, Arun ran behind them too.

George stopped in the middle of the hall and shouted at the top of his voice, “Damn it, I knew this would happen. That is why I told you to stay away from him.”

"It is just a minor confusion," Esha pleaded, trying to make him understand, "Granny was not wearing her spectacles. She thought Arun was you, that's all. It is nothing."

George then turned towards Arun and rushed forward to grab his collar. "You" he growled, "you are trying to act too smart, but remember, she is mine."

Esha tried to break them apart, but George was far too strong and in no mood to listen to her either. He pushed her out of the way and started blaming her for everything.

Arun was furious seeing Esha being treated that way by someone who was supposed to protect her and spend the rest of his life with her. Unable to control himself, he retaliated, slamming George against a pillar. Holding him by his neck, Arun said threateningly, "You better behave nicely with her. Just because she remains quiet doesn't mean you can say anything to her. If you hurt her, I will kill you."

George was taken by surprise at this sudden burst of anger and stood still. Arun soon recovered and felt everybody's dumbstruck gaze on them. Esha stood in a corner, crying quietly on Priyanka's shoulder. He let go of George in disgust and walked over to Esha. In a broken voice, he said, "I'm sorry, I should not have come here. I'll leave now. You take care of yourself."

He left with tears in his eyes. It was torturous for him to walk away from Esha when she was so distressed, but he could not stay there any longer.

Not wanting to be by himself that day, he went to Rohit's apartment. They stayed up drinking and keeping each other company, though not talking much. Suddenly, Rohit's phone rang. It was Esha, asking about Arun's whereabouts. "I'll be there in thirty minutes," she said.

Thinking that it wasn't a good idea for them to meet again, Arun said aloud, "I don't want to be the reason behind any more tension for her. I'll leave."

Rohit pulled him down and said, "Are you mad? She needs you the most right now. She must feel so terrible about everything that happened, and you are running away."

Arun felt on edge, and paced up and down, wondering how Esha would react. She came in, her hair loose, her eyes puffy and threw her hands around him to hug him. He held her tightly and looked at Rohit over her shoulder, feeling helpless against her streaming tears.

They murmured words of comfort to her. Rohit said, "Don't cry, you are a strong girl. We are always there for you. Do you want us to give that doctor a strong beating and tighten his loosened screws?"

"Not required. I dealt with him already and broke off my engagement with him," she said between sobs and looked up at them. Overlooking their stunned expressions, she sighed, "Shall we go for a bike ride, guys? I badly need some fresh air."

They went out into the night, riding the empty streets of

the city, letting the cool breeze calm their thoughts. As soon as they came back, Rohit took their leave to go inside and sleep. Only then did Arun ask her the question that had been eating him up from inside all this while. “Why did you break off your engagement?” he asked. “He was to be your future.”

Esha started at the ground, taking her time to process her thoughts and put them into the most appropriate words, “After you left, I couldn’t stop crying over everything that had happened. George, instead of apologising, told me that you are not a good person and that you’re just trying to draw my attention towards you and break up my engagement. He told me to stay away from you.”

“And then?” he prompted when she fell silent.

She gazed at him steadily and said, “And then I told him to stay away from me. How dare you try to pick a fight, I asked him. It was just a small confusion and you turned it into such a big scene. I told him that I would be a fool to marry him, and then threw the engagement ring at him.”

Arun was in awe of the strong and beautiful girl in front of him. Touched, he gave her a hug and asked, “How does it feel to have broken things off with him?”

Esha finally smiled a little, blinked and said, “It feels nice. I feel free.”

They sat together, had a drink, and continued to talk about all sorts of things. It was late when she turned to him and asked, “What about you? Did you find a suitable girl?”

Arun breathed out a hollow laughter. His search for a suitable girl had been a very complicated story. He leaned back and contemplated the idea of telling Esha all about it. He said, "Maybe you can tell me if I am right in my perspective or not. See, there was this girl in my office that I liked a lot and we were happy with our relationship. One day, while working late on a project, she tried to kiss me. I pulled back. It was just not the right place for me. She broke things off right away, saying that we were very different in our thinking."

He paused to pour himself a drink, and then continued, "Another time, I became friends with another colleague while working together with her. She invited me out to a pub with her friends. While dancing, she moved closer and tried to kiss me. I couldn't bring myself to do it. We had only been friends till then. And we haven't spoken since… Tell me Esha, am I wrong in thinking that these intimate moments are very special, and that there is a proper time and place for them?"

Esha looked at him sympathetically. "Oh Arun, you are not wrong at all." She moved forward to take his face in the palm of her hands and making him look at her, she said, "You are a gem of a person. You'll find so many girls who would want to be in a relationship with a guy like you. God has made a special person for everyone. You just need to find the one for you."

"Why is it that only you understand me so well?" he said, hugging her close to himself.

She melted into his arms. He felt an electric energy flowing between them. Her heart was beating in sync with his and her warmth seeped into his very soul. They stayed like that for some time, breathing silently, and for the first time in his life, Arun felt completely at ease.

He pulled away slightly to look at her face and his heart started to beat faster. She looked captivating; her lips were slightly parted, her eyes dark with emotion, and her skin burned under his touch. Her soft fingers brushing his cheeks overwhelmed him. Instinctively, he cradled her face in his hands and leaned forward to kiss her. Her lips felt soft and sweet under his, and the kiss deepened as she laced her fingers through his hair.

The spell suddenly broke when he felt Esha pushing him away. With a bit of struggle, they broke off and sat staring at each other. She shifted awkwardly, scrambled to gather her purse and left the apartment hurriedly.

He lay awake for hours, dreaming about Esha and trying to understand his own feelings towards her. Unable to take it anymore when morning came, he called her to apologise. As soon as she answered the call, he blurted out, "I am sorry for last night. It just happened before I could understand what I was doing..."

She cut him off and said, "Arun, I will call you later."

He heard the click at the other end and put the phone away slowly. 'She must be angry,' he thought, 'Maybe it is better if she takes some time to think things through.'

He spent the entire day hoping and waiting for her call. He had to know what was on her mind. When the call finally came, she confessed, "George called my parents last night and apologised for creating such a scene. He was here in the morning when you called."

"So, are you back with him now?" he asked, even though he already knew her answer.

He heard her take a deep breath before saying, "I have no choice. Everybody likes him and they think he is good for me. Whatever I am doing is for my family."

He could barely process her words. Feeling empty and broken all over again, he said, "Take care, Esha. Goodbye."

He could not think nor function anymore. He took a break from work for a few days and locked himself up in his room. He tried to sleep, but strange thoughts kept hovering through his mind. Awake and alone, he made himself a drink. Soon he found himself drinking all the time. His thoughts churned constantly in his brain. Was Esha making the right decision? Would she be happy? Was he going to lose his friend forever?

Drowsy and lightheaded, he lay on the floor one night, staring at chips of paint peeling off the ceiling. His mind wandered to the time he was at the beach with Esha. The way the moon had reflected on the surface of the sea wonderfully enhanced the beauty of the night. He closed his eyes, remembering how she had splashed the sea water at him and how he had chased her, her squeals of laughter echoing in the night.

In his wakeful dream, he caught hold of her slender waist and turned her around to face him. She looked radiant in the moonlight. He pulled her close and pressed his lips against her soft ones.

Just then, some people appeared from the darkness and held him back. Although he fought with all his strength, Esha was dragged away from him to a Jeep. It took off into the jungle and he ran after it. Her voice bellowed in the distance, "Arun, save me…I love you, Arun. I have always loved you."

"Esha, I love you! Don't go," he shouted back, trying to keep up. The Jeep disappeared into darkness, while he fell to the ground and kept crying, "Esha…Esha…come back. I love you. I can't live without you."

Desperately he screamed "Esha!" and his eyes flew open. He sprang up, looking around the dark room wildly. Realising it was only a dream, he sank back onto his bed, drenched in sweat and breathing heavily. All his fears about losing Esha had manifested themselves in his dream. He felt completely helpless without her. He hung his head in his hands, coming to the realisation that he was in love with her. 'All these years, it had only been Esha on my mind. She was the one I always loved,' he thought.

'It is too late,' he despaired, 'She is getting married to

George.' In his heart however, he knew that if he didn't tell her now how he felt, he would never be able to forgive himself.

He got up, grabbed the keys of his bike and left the house, not even bothering to change out of his crumpled shirt. It was only after he reached Esha's house that he looked at his watch and noted the time. It was 3 A.M. and he stopped himself in time from ringing the doorbell.

Instead, he sat on his bike and tried to figure out exactly what he should say to her. Minutes ticked by slowly and as it neared 5 A.M., he left in search of a local phone booth. In all his hurry to get there, he had forgotten his cellphone at home.

Her phone kept ringing for a long time and just when he was going to give up, Esha answered.

"Esha?" he whispered, his mouth dry.

"Arun…? What happened? Why are you calling me at this hour? Is something wrong?" She asked, her voice still groggy with sleep.

He steeled his nerves and said, "I need to talk to you. I am outside your house. Can you meet me? Right now?"

Something in the tone of his voice must have made her realise that it was important because she immediately got alert and said, "I will be out in 5 minutes."

He waited impatiently, wanting to get it over with before he changed his mind. She soon came out of the gate, wrapped up in a shawl. The sight of her made him want to hug her, but he stopped himself.

"Is everything okay? Please tell me quickly, you're driving me crazy with worry," she said.

He couldn't find the right words and simply said, "Can we go to some place? I just need to talk to you."

"You are scaring me, Arun," she said, her face scrunched up with tension, "Come on, there is a tea shop around the corner, we can go there."

They walked the short distance together and sat down next to each other on the long bench. He closed his eyes and tried to steady his voice. "I found the girl I want to spend the rest of my life with," he said in a breath.

Esha's encouraging smile faltered a little. "Nice," she said slowly, "who is she?"

He looked at her and said softly, "She is everything that I have ever wanted. She is kind hearted, strong, and beautiful. I am amazed by her every second of every day. She brings out the best in me. I don't know what love is, but I have never felt such a strong connection with anyone besides her."

She averted her eyes and turned to face the road, a pained expression on her face.

He continued, "Esha…the girl is you. You make me feel things I have never felt before. I have missed living like this through all these years that we have been apart."

She looked at him, took his hand in hers and entwined her fingers through his. "Arun, you are my best friend," she said, "I have shared some of the best moments of my life with you. But there is nothing more than friendship in my heart for you."

He swallowed her words and tried to pull his hand away. She smiled sadly and watched him, "What happened between us that day, didn't mean anything. Both of us were lonely and vulnerable and we got carried away. It was a mistake. We have a special friendship. I hope you understand this and not give up on our friendship."

"Never…you are the best thing I have in my life," he choked out, "I cannot lose you. Our friendship is very precious to me."

They sat there wordlessly for a few minutes. Arun felt heavy while his eyes swam with tears. Esha stood up as the sun began to rise and walked away saying that she needed to be home. He was left alone with a broken heart.

Chapter 9

He kept his heartbreak to himself, never bringing it up, even to Rohit or his mother. Esha's words that he was no more than a best friend, pained his heart. He took on extra work at office to keep his mind occupied. He worked odd hours and through the weekends, coming home only to sleep when he was exhausted. He knew it was not healthy for him, but work was a welcome distraction. He could not bear the thought of Esha in his mind all the time.

One day, tired and distracted, he was heading towards a client's office on his bike when a car came speeding around the corner and directly at him. He tried to swerve around, but his reaction was too slow and he crashed into it. The bike flew into the air and he landed on the road a few feet away, knocked unconscious.

He woke up to the cold white lights of his hospital room. His head felt sore and the doctor informed him that he had received several stitches. He had to stay in the hospital under observation for a few days.

"You are lucky you did not sustain heavy injuries. I have told uncle and aunty not to worry. Esha and I are here to take care of you," said Rohit when he came to visit. Esha sat quietly beside him, pale and drawn. She came every day, but things were not the same between them anymore. There was less talk and laughter, and it was left to Rohit to carry forward all conversation.

He wanted to get out of the hospital and get away from her as soon as possible. The hurt was still fresh and he needed some space to heal. On the day of his discharge, Rohit went to take care of the paperwork, while Esha insisted on waiting with Arun. A nurse came by and handed Arun the bills for his treatment.

"Give them to me," said Esha, "I'll keep them with me until Rohit comes for them. They must have missed him at the reception."

Arun nodded and lay back on his bed. An awkward silence filled the room. He felt relieved when she stepped out to answer a call.

Rohit peered in, "Did they bring the bills here?"

Arun replied, "Yes, Esha kept them in her purse. Just check, she has stepped out for a call."

He watched disinterestedly as Rohit rooted through the purse.

"Ah, here they are," he said, pulling out a sheaf of papers. A small card got pulled out along with the rest of the papers and landed by his feet. Rohit bent down to pick it up. He straightened up slowly, looking closely at the piece of paper.

"What happened? Arun asked, "What's that?"

Rohit silently handed him the card. He took it and turned it over. It was a picture of him and Esha from school. He noticed immediately that it had been cut out of their class photograph to show just the two of them. There was a red heart drawn across it, enclosing both of their faces.

He looked up at the sound of Esha entering the room and gazed at her questioningly, not paying attention to Rohit slipping out of the room. Extending his arm, he handed the photograph to Esha and waited expectantly for her reply.

Esha looked a little apprehensive. Slowly, she came towards him and sat on the edge of his bed. She said, "I didn't realise when you took up a special place in my heart. I cried the whole night when you left for Nagpur. That is when I cut out this picture to keep with me. I waited to meet you all those years. I prayed, but there was no response from you. I thought you had forgotten all about me. It was difficult, but I just had to meet you once again, so I planned the alumni meet. I couldn't control my excitement, but I had to keep my distance. I did not want you to love me just because I loved you."

He smiled at her and said, "Just like the seashore?"

She started to cry, "I love you but I cannot marry you, Arun."

But why, he wanted to scream. He struggled to comprehend her words.

She wiped her tears and continued, "I was four years old when I was adopted from the Sunshine Orphanage. My parents showered me with love and affection. They sent me to the best schools, encouraged me to participate in all kinds of activities and supported all my dreams. Granny once told me that they did not want me to feel left out so they never had a child of their own. I have never told this to anyone before because I have never felt like an orphan living with my family. I can never hope to pay them back for what they have done for me."

He felt bad for doubting her reasoning earlier. He gathered her into a hug and let her sob against his chest. Gently stroked her back to sooth her, he said, "Shh! You are a strong girl. Don't cry, Esha. I am always there for you. I understand that your parents are important to you and you want to make them happy by marrying George. I respect your decision."

He did understand. At least his Esha did love him back, but it did not help make his heart feel any less heavy. Instead, it made his love and respect for her grow all the more.

Much too soon, the day of her wedding arrived and he still did not have his emotions under control. 'It is a big day for Esha and I cannot miss it,' he told himself sternly in the mirror.

His mother heard the pain in his voice as she passed him by. She, along with his father, had come down to the city for Esha's wedding too, not knowing anything about Arun's emotional turmoil. She drew closer to hug him and he rested his head on her shoulder. In her embrace, all his barriers broke down and he spilled out everything to her.

Arun's mother, calm as always, said, "You can never predict how things are going to work out. Keep your faith."

He sought a hollow comfort in her words. The wedding was in a Church and for the first time in his life, he kneeled to pray before Jesus. He took his seat then and waited for the bride to arrive.

The time finally came and music swelled through the hall. Heart thumping wildly in his chest, he turned around to watch Esha step through the wooden doors into the church. She walked down the aisle on her father's arm, her hair tied to one side, and the train of her white gown trailing behind her.

He could not take his eyes off her. He willed her to look at him one last time and soon, his prayers were heard. She raised her downcast eyes off the ground and turned them to look at him. Hesitantly, she slowed down as she passed him, tears blurring her vision.

He wanted to put his hand out and hold hers. He wanted to stop her, but her father tugged her onward. She stumbled and turned to face ahead again. Looking so beautiful, she was walking away from him and towards George, who was standing at the altar.

Arun sat down slowly, his heart aching and his eyes brimming with unshed tears. A certain ringing in his head made everybody, except for Esha, fade away. He wanted to run out of the Church, but he couldn't move.

He noticed her looking back at him every few seconds, even as the priest cleared his throat and started to speak. Their eyes locked and they stared at each other, oblivious to the crowd that had started whispering and wondering, giving rise to an uncomfortable buzz in the Church. The Priest paused, mystified by the unusual scene. George took Esha's hand and jerked it his way to make her look at him. She tore her hand out of his grasp and pushed him away.

Arun watched astounded, as she threw back her veil and ran towards him. He wiped his tears, stood up and hardly heard the collective horrified gasp as they fell into each other's arms. Esha shuddered and whispered repeatedly, "I love you, Arun. I love you. I cannot marry anyone else."

He wiped her tears away with his cold quivering hands and said, "And I love you, Esha. I love you so much."

Arun felt a strong grip on his shoulder, roughly pulling

him back. Before George could land a punch, Esha's father stopped him and said, "Let it be, son. She is no longer my daughter." Esha's father turned to face the gathering and continued, "I'm sorry for this mess. There is no longer a wedding taking place here."

The confused buzzing escalated and the guests filed out slowly, trying to comprehend what had just happened. Esha's eyes were red and all the kohl around them had spread over her cheeks, running down with her tears. She approached her father and cried, "I'm sorry, Dad." She tried to hug him but he pushed away in disgust and turned to leave. It broke Arun's heart to watch the exchange.

"Please, they have loved each other since their school days," Arun's mother stepped forward to plead with him, "Forgive her, she is your child."

"She is no child of mine and she has proved it to me today," Esha's father snarled. He grabbed his wife's hand and walked towards the Church's exit. Esha's mother turned around to look at her daughter one last time. Their gazes met and Esha fell to her knees wailing inconsolably. Arun gathered her up and took her back home along with his parents.

She spent the next few days calling home, but nobody would speak to her anymore. Arun knew he could not do anything for her and simply held her while she cried.

Arun's family decided to have a small court wedding for them as soon as possible. His parents went to Esha's house to invite her family, but returned disheartened. Esha had spent the day on the balcony, waiting eagerly for some silver lining, but seeing the expression on Arun's parents' faces, she withdrew into the room and locked herself in.

Arun hurried to ask his mother what had happened. She told him how Esha's father had turned them away, saying that he could not give his blessings to a person who did not care about the family or its reputation. He did not want to be bothered about Esha anymore.

Arun was disappointed with their reaction. He had hoped for them to come around, it meant so much to Esha to have the support of her parents. The day of their wedding dawned bright and clear, but they still hadn't heard anything from Esha's family.

It was Arun's mother who dressed Esha and gifted her a beautiful diamond necklace to wear on her special day. When he saw her all dressed up, as she walked into the room, his eyes widening with appreciation for his lovely bride-to-be. Rohit nudged him and he laughed, hardly able to believe that he was going to marry Esha.

At the court, a few other of their friends joined them. Esha was a little subdued all through. She looked around now and then, constantly checking the doorway whenever she heard anybody walk in, hoping it to be her parents.

"Come Esha, let's go inside," Arun said gently when their names were called out. "Everybody is waiting for us."

She glanced around, hoping to see her parents one last time, before giving up completely and following him inside. It was a simple procedure. The Registrar asked them for their papers and ID proofs, and made them sign a declaration.

Arun took Esha's hands in his, slipped a ring onto her finger and said, "I, Arun Shetty, take Esha Williams to be my lawful wife."

Esha looked up at him shyly and said, "And I, Esha Williams, take Arun Shetty to be my lawful husband."

Their friends cheered and he felt tears prickling the back of his eyes. His parents and Rohit signed the marriage certificate as witnesses, and just like that it was over. They were married.

He leaned forward and whispered in Esha's ear, "Congratulations, my best friend, or should I say congratulations, my wife. I'm so lucky I get to have both in you."

She blushed and threw him a huge smile.

Together they received the good wishes of all their friends. His mother came forward and hugged Esha, kissing her on the forehead. Bursting with happiness, Arun put his arms around them both and teased, "Don't forget about me, now that you have Esha for a daughter."

The small gathering then moved to a park near his house where his parents had organised a party for the newly married couple, having invited all their friends, relatives and colleagues. They had the trees and the park gate decorated with lights and had set up musical arrangements. He watched Esha look around in wonder, glowing prettily, with her hand firmly clasped in his.

She looked at him and he felt moved by the look of adoration on her face. As a new song started, he twirled her around and she laughed. The celebratory mood was crackling up nicely and the guests slowly started coming forward in pairs to dance to the lovely music.

Some of their school friends said teasing, "We knew there was something between the two of you since school!" Arun and Esha gazed happily into each other's eyes.

Suddenly, there heard a commotion at the entrance. A man in a crumpled shirt pushed his way through the crowd. When Arun's father moved to stop him, he protested, "I have come to meet Esha Madam."

Arun looked at Esha to see if she knew him. She stepped into the light and came forward. "Shyam Singh!' she exclaimed in surprise, "What are you doing here? Is everyone at home okay? Is no one going to come to my wedding party?"

The man shook his head sadly, "No Madam, no one is coming. I am here because Granny sent me. She wanted you to have this." He handed her a small box.

Arun watched with the rest of the guests as Esha extended a trembling hand and took the box. She opened it to reveal a small silver figurine of Jesus and a pretty pair of gold earrings. A piece of paper tumbled out. Arun picked it up and handed it to her.

She moved her lips, silently forming the words she was reading, "God bless you, my child. Love you, my darling."

She folded the paper, bought it to her lips, and kissed it. There was small peace to be found in Granny's gift.

Later that evening, when they had settled down in their room after the party, Esha put on the earrings and peered into the mirror to check her reflection.

Arun, who was standing in the doorway, looked at her keenly. She looked happy. He went up to her and put his hands on her shoulders. "They look very pretty on you," he said softly, kissing her cheek.

Her face lit up and she turned around and moved closer, intertwining her arms with his.

"Come," he said, "I know somewhere nice where we can sit."

He led her to the terrace of his apartment. From there, they had a clear view of the park still lit up, post the celebration of their marriage. There they sat down, at level with the tree tops glittering with lights. Her hair shone under the moonlight as he played with it. He said, "I had never believed in prayers until today. I always thought a man should live each day as it comes to him. But I didn't have the strength to watch you leave me. I was lost without you. I think Mom was always correct, you should never leave hope."

She rested her head on his shoulder and sighed, "You know, I was so restless the day I was to get married to George. I closed my eyes and felt as if you were with me for a moment . But then you disappeared and I was on my own again. Loneliness engulfed me. When I saw you at the Church, I froze. I felt as if I was committing a sin marrying another man."

It had been a painful realisation for both of them. He just hummed in response and put his arm around her, holding her close. Suddenly, she broke into a giggle. "What is so funny?" he asked her with a smile.

"The two girls you told me about, the ones who tried to kiss you, are they Rhea and Adiya?" she asked, sitting up straight.

He raised his eyebrows in surprise. "Yes," he said slowly, "how do you know, anyway?"

"You are a lucky girl. It is very difficult to find people like Arun," she imitated and said grinning, "Both of them told me that."

He laughed and reached out to take her face in his hands. He said, "I only wanted to kiss the one who is permanently on my mind."

She blushed and brought her face up to his. For a

moment, they looked at each other dreamily, the answer to their prayers right in front of them. As a sweet song drifted through the night, their lips met in a kiss and they melted into each other.

Chapter 10

They named their place Arusha.

"That is going to be the name of our baby girl," Esha told him as they settled into the new house. She was sure that once they had a baby, her parents' heart would soften and they would accept their union.

He hoped that she was right and laughed along with all her plans. A baby with Esha had been no less than a dream and he could not wait for it to come true.

They set about decorating the house, constantly planning their future and wondering what all it had in store for them. Their new house was small and cosy, and they filled it with love and laughter. Esha set up a corner with candles and photographs of them with their families. She placed fresh flowers in vases, organised a shelf with all their favourite books, and made the place really feel like a perfect home.

It was surprisingly easy how they fell into routine, taking turns to get up early in the morning to make breakfast and pack their respective tiffins for office. While he was always sleepy and rushed about to get to work on time, Esha made time to do her prayers and feed the birds at the window every morning before leaving for work.

Sundays were special days that they kept for themselves. On the first Sunday at their new home, Arun was woken up by Esha snuggling against him and kissing him good morning. He made them some tea and they spent an hour cuddling in bed, talking about their week. He could think of no better way to spend a Sunday.

Sometimes, she would insist on him to do his prayers too, but he ignored it. To such requests, he responded with a smile, saying, "I've got you. I don't need anything else."

They were very happy together. Despite some small fights here and there, neither of them could stay angry with the other for very long. They would quickly apologise and make up. They never missed a chance to say, "I love you" or to hold each other tight. Although, beneath her infectious smile, he knew that she harboured the pain of being disowned by her parents. Sometimes, he found her eyes becoming distant and she would fall silent. He tried to be there for her at such times. His mother sensed her pain too and called them often to speak to Esha. To her, Esha was as good as her own daughter.

It was almost their second wedding anniversary when Esha finally conceived. The two lines displayed on the pregnancy test kit changed their lives. They were ecstatic when they found out. A baby of their own! Esha kept the pregnancy test kit safe as a memento.

The next day, Esha insisted that they go shopping for the baby. Arun watched her as she picked up accessories to decorate the baby's room. He helped her as far as he could, sharing equally Esha's excitement about the baby. That night when they returned home, Esha and Arun decorated a spare room for the baby, inspite of being terribly tired.

When they were done, Esha sat down beside Arun and sighed, "I feel so blessed."

Arun nodded his head and said, "Me too."

"You know what? I wish we have a daughter," Esha said and looked at Arun, her eyes glittering.

Arun enveloped Esha in a hug and said, "I too want a daughter who is just as cute, smart and adorable like you. I can't wait to have a little one just like you here."

Both of them drifted off to sleep that night talking about their first baby and wondering how different their lives would get once the baby arrives.

Their joy, however, was short lived. Esha miscarried in the second month of her pregnancy. The doctor assured them that it could happen to anyone and said, "Keep trying, everything is fine." But stories of miscarriage by their friends and relatives triggered Esha's restless mind. The fear of not becoming a mother crept into her heart. She started visiting Sunshine Orphanage, where she had spent her early years at. He would watch her leave the house with a sore heart everyday but the time spent with children there seemed to lessen her grief.

They did not give up trying. Arun and Esha met with various doctors over the months and tried multiple fertility treatments, but their destiny was against them. Esha was shattered. She had pinned all her hopes on a baby, not just because she badly wanted a child, but also because the child would have given her a chance to mend relations with her parents.

As a result, she withdrew completely and even stopped going to work for a while. She stopped taking care of herself and became disinterested in everything that used to give her pleasure before. Arun was consumed with worry. Nothing he said consoled her or made any difference. He knew he could live without a baby, but not without Esha.

One day, on the way back from work, he bought a dog on impulse. He came home and handed him over to Esha tentatively. She held the little puppy in her arms and gently stroked him. At last, she looked up and smiled for the first time in weeks, and said, "I'm going to call him Rambo." He sighed with relief.

The puppy seemed to draw her out of her sadness little by little. She played with him all day long, taking him for long walks, giving him baths, and snuggling with him in bed. She showered all her love on Rambo, and in turn, he followed her everywhere, licking her face and making her laugh.

Once, they were walking on the beach when she finally spoke to him about all her pain and insecurities. Her eyes fixed on their lengthening shadows, she said, "Why is this happening to us?"

He clasped her hand tightly in his own and drew it closer to his chest, "These are testing times. We can't lose hope now. We have to face them together. Our love is strong enough to deal with whatever comes our way."

He could see that she was not convinced. She looked pensively at a little boy playing with his mother, further down the beach from them. She turned towards Arun and voiced her fear aloud, "Is it because I betrayed my parents that such a pain has come my way as punishment?"

"Are you mad?" he almost shouted, "Look Esha, however angry your parents might be, they would never hold anything bad against you in their hearts. You have to remember that."

Her words, however, wormed their way into his mind. 'It is I, who is responsible for all her pain,' he pondered all night and fell into an uneasy sleep.

The next morning, he woke up early to make tea and came back to sit on the bed, watching Esha sleep. She had lost all her glow; there were dark patches under her eyes, her sky was dry, her lips chapped, her hair tangled, and her body looked weak. Even her sleep was disturbed, she tossed about often, shifting from side to side. It pained Arun to watch her in that state. He wondered what he could do to bring back the real Esha.

She suddenly woke up with a jerk. Her eyes fell on the clock and she jumped up saying, "It's so late, why didn't you wake me before?"

"It is Sunday, you are not late for anything. Here, drink some tea," he replied with a small but warm smile. "Esha, let's start again."

She took a sip and looked puzzled, "What do you want to start again?"

He cupped her cheek in the palm of his hand and said, "Let's go meet your parents. We will request them to forgive us. It is not just your burden to bear. I feel just as responsible, and I am equally liable to ask them for forgiveness."

Her eyes brightened instantaneously. "Really?" she asked.

"Really," he smiled back, "We should go."

She sat there for a moment, thrilled at the idea of seeing her parents again. But soon, some harsh realisation dawned on her that eclipsed her smile and she said, "I have been calling them for more than two years now and they always hang up before I am even able to say anything. I don't think they will forgive us. What is the point of going?"

"We have to keep trying, Esha," he said, aching for her to feel whole again.

She smiled again. Looking at him with eyes full of affection, she said, "I love you."

She took her time to get ready, asking him which dress to wear and whether she should tie her hair back or not.

The entire journey, Esha fidgeted with her hair and restlessly looked out the car window. Arun patted her hand softly and told her to relax. It was mid-morning when they reached her parents' house. He took her hand and asked, "Ready?"

She nodded her head quickly and pressed on the bell. They waited nervously, slightly perspiring under the hot sun. Esha's mother opened the door and froze in her tracks. "Esha?" she whispered dazed, "Oh, my Esha, how are you? I missed you so much."

Arun stepped back as Esha fell into her mother's arms and buried her face in her neck. The sound of the two women weeping must have carried inside because her father soon appeared in the hallway. His face turned red and distorted with anger when he spotted them at the door, and he shouted at his wife, "What is all this drama going on? Come inside right away and shut the door!"

Esha's mother drew back, tears streaming down her

cheeks and reluctantly closed the door on them.

"No…Mom, Dad, please forgive me," Esha hammered on the door and cried.

There was no answer. Arun could not understand how they could ignore their daughter's pleas in such a cruel way. Wiping tears from under his own eyes, he supported her up from where she had slid down the door onto the ground and took her home.

The visit had broken whatever little hope she had of reconciling with her parents. From that day on, she went around like a lost soul, going through the motions of everyday life but not really feeling anything. Arun couldn't forgive himself for being the reason behind such torment. He regretted taking her to her parent's house.

A few days later, Arun received a call from Esha's workplace, informing him that Esha had collapsed at work. He had feared something like that to happen. He reached there as fast as he could, a bad feeling lingering at the back of his mind.

The doctor ordered x-rays and admitted her for some tests immediately. "Don't worry, I'm fine," she kept trying to reassure him, but he couldn't shake off the feeling that something was terribly wrong. He remembered how disturbed her sleep used to be and goose bumps ran up his arms. 'Please, let me be wrong,' he prayed, leaning his head back against the wall.

A nurse appeared to summon him inside. He wanted to scream and let out all his angst, but he forced himself to sit down across the doctor and listen to what he had to say.

"Mr Shetty..." the doctor regarded him gravely through his spectacles, "I'm afraid Esha has, what is essentially, a malignant brain tumour. We have examined her scans and I regret to inform you that it has grown to such an advanced stage that there is no cure or treatment for her. I am very sorry."

His ears rang with a sudden rush of sounds. Arun felt closely the exact moment when the world fell apart for him while he sat there, his mouth open in a silent scream of denial.

He walked back to Esha's room in a state of shock. 'There is no hope,' the doctor's words played in his head over and over again. His mind felt numb to all human emotions. He felt as if time had started testing him again by threatening to take Esha away from him. He watched Esha sleep, her face wan and bleary with exhaustion. 'I have to find a cure, I have to find a way for us to fight this,' he resolved.

It was a frantic battle. He formulated a hurried plan to approach various hospitals and spent the next few days running from one doctor to another, hoping to receive some assurance from somewhere that they would be able to take up her case and handle the matter.

His parents flew down to support them too. While his mother spent the day sitting with Esha, his father called up his contacts and forwarded Esha's case file to specialists all across the country. However, there was no positive response from anyone.

Meanwhile, Esha's condition worsened with each passing day. The doctors could do no more than try to contain her pain and make her feel comfortable.

"Take me home, Arun. I want to be home with you. I don't like it here," she said one day, catching hold of his hand. He looked at her helplessly, knowing that all his efforts had failed. Only their prayers could save her from there.

He went to the doctors with her request and by the end of the next day, Esha was back at their house in their bed. She told him that it created a sense of normalcy for her, but in reality, their house had been stripped off of all its coziness and was converted to look like a mini hospital itself.

There were tubes set up in their bedroom for Esha's medication and a nurse was arranged to visit her every day. Arun's mother stayed with them to help, preparing fresh soups and vegetables each day, and making sure that everything was taken care of.

As his mother fed Esha that first night back at home, Arun leaned against the doorway, unnoticed by them, and listened to them talking.

Esha said, "I should be the one to take care of you. Our destinies are so twisted that a mother is taking care of a daughter."

His mother gently brushed Esha's hair away from her face and said, "We are a family. All of us are meant to take care of each other."

Esha took his mother's hand in her own and smiled tearfully, "I am blessed to have a mother like you. But in this life, God has gifted me with a very short time with you."

"Each moment with you is special for me. I had never experienced the love of a daughter until you became a part of my life." He could hear the love and concern colouring her voice as she said, "And now, I don't want you to cry anymore."

He walked into the room just as Esha finished her food and laid back down. She turned to look at him and said softly to his mother, "God has been very kind to have given me you and Arun in my life."

His mother smiled, clearing the tray of food, and carrying it out of the room.

Arun took her place by Esha's side and held her hand. "Go to sleep, you need to rest," he said.

She shook her head and said, "I want to see you. I want to feel you holding me."

He had had a long day which left him feeling drained and emotional. Without a word, he climbed onto the bed beside her, kissed her forehead and held her close till she fell asleep.

The next morning, he woke up to find Esha struggling to get out of bed. Quickly, he sprang up to help her, "Where are you going? You should have woken me up."

She pointed to the window and said, "The birds will be waiting for me. I feed them every day and they always come at this time. Will you get some wheat grains from the kitchen? See, the sparrow is already here."

He shook his head at her. Only she could be so considerate about little things like that, even while their whole world was falling apart. He fetched the grains from the kitchen and sat her down by the window. It was a peaceful morning and he wished for time to just stop, so he could capture the perfect moment of them sitting by the birds, early in the morning.

But the days passed by rapidly, bringing more change into their lives as Esha's health deteriorated. He was unwilling to leave her even for a minute. Work and office were forgotten completely, as he focused all his effort on looking after Esha.

One day, Esha noticed red sores all over her body. Her face tightened with pain as she tried to move. Arun was moved to tears just watching her. He turned his face away before she could see him.

"You have started hiding things from me now?" she said sadly.

He looked up and attempted a smile. "No Esha, I feel so helpless at not being able to take away your pain."

She opened her arms towards him, inviting him in for a hug. He allowed her to cradle him and cried into her neck. She stroked his back and said, "Shh... the sickness doesn't hurt me as much as it does to see you cry."

She cupped his face in both her hands and made him look at her, "Arun, you have to be strong. You have to promise me that you will never let go of hope to live your life to the fullest."

He refused to meet her eyes, "I can't."

"Do you want me to leave you crying? I want to cherish each moment that I have left with you. If you don't promise to take care of yourself, I will die worrying about you."

He looked up at her then and said fiercely, "No, you are not leaving me. You're not going anywhere. That's it! No more discussions!"

His mother walked into the room just then. He shouted, "Ma, tell her not to bring up the topic of dying."

Esha tried to calm him down and said, "Okay, okay I will never say that again. Now, I'm hungry. Will you get me something to eat?"

Taking a deep breath, he took a hold of his emotions and went out to get her some food.

He could evade the reality momentarily, but it did not change the fact that Esha was indeed dying and there was nothing they could do about it.

Her pain turned so severe that one morning, she woke up crying, "My head feels like someone is digging a hole in it. Make it stop!"

Frightened, Arun called the doctors. As they worked, he sat next to her, begging God to spare her life and make her better.

She did not remove her gaze from his face all through. Even as the doctors injected her with more pain medication, she managed to get up halfway from her bed to reach for him. Putting her cold hand against his cheek, she said, "You are the best thing that has ever happened to me. I promised that I will always be with you, but I cannot take it anymore. I will always love you. You have given me so much happiness. I want you to be happy now… Arun, this pain is unbearable… please free me."

Choked with crying, he tried to hold her fragile form tenderly against his own self. She lay her head against his shoulder and whispered, "Arun, I can't."

Tears streamed thickly down his face and he helped her lie back down on the bed. She looked at him weakly and tried to smile, "I love you."

"I love you, Esha," he said, his voice heavy with emotion. He couldn't do anything but watch as her eyes shut slowly, a ghost of a smile still playing on her face.

The Doctor came forward to feel her pulse and shook his head. Arun's senses seemed to be failing him. He could see the Doctor's lips move as he said the words, 'I am sorry, but Esha is no more,' but he did not react. Tears continued to flow silently down his face and he did not know for how long he stood there, simply looking at Esha's peaceful form, finally at rest.

After

Chapter 11

Arun walked along the beach, his hands deep in his pockets, looking fixedly at the setting sun. The sky was a fiery orange and it reminded him of another sunset on another beach, a year ago. Esha's warm hand had held his and he had been happy. Now, he was alone, convinced that he would never feel joy ever again.

He turned to head back home, knowing that his mother would be waiting for him with food. He preempted how she would scold him for not telling her when he left the house that morning, or for his messy clothes and overgrown hair. He knew that she was worried about him and only wanted to take care of him, just as she used to when he was a child.

'But I am not a child anymore,' he thought bitterly. 'My wife is dead and nobody can take away the void that has been left inside me.'

Shifting to Goa was supposed to make it easier for him to start afresh. Yet, a year had passed and he was still living as though in transit; an empty house, no job, and depending on his mother to take care of everything. He felt bereft and desolate, All his mother's prayers to Esha's soul changed nothing.

While wandering around that day, he noticed a group of people gathered around a small cross of Jesus at the end of the beach, lighting candles around it. He was about to walk past it without stopping to find out what was happening, when a small boy sprang up in front of him and said, "Uncle, would you like to light a candle in front of Jesus? It is Easter today."

He shook his head, trying to brush past and move away from the crowd, but the boy didn't give up. "My mom says we should always pray, even if we don't feel like praying. Prayers create miracles," the boy said.

Arun looked at the boy, suddenly recalling how Esha used to tell him to pray all the time and how he never listened to her.

He felt as if some strange force was dragging him closer towards the statue. The boy smiled and handed him a candle.

Arun prayed in his heart, "Three years ago you blessed me by bringing Esha back into my life. Then, when everything started to feel like a dream, you took her away. Today, I have nothing left in my life that can give me the strength to live on. I just want to be with Esha again. I cannot stay away from her."

A strange peaceful sensation swept through his body, spreading through his arms and down to his feet, lingering on even after his prayer had ended.

"Arun, where are you going? Come and eat your dinner," his mother's voice called out predictably as he tried to sneak past her to his room when he got back.

"I'm not hungry, Ma," he said, suddenly exhausted. If only he could go to sleep and be back with Esha in his dreams.

She grabbed his arm and said, "If you don't eat, then I won't eat either."

It was a regular argument and he knew how adamant his mother could get. Sighing, he sat down at the table and let her serve him.

"Eat up, I have something to show you after dinner," she said, a quiet excitement in her voice.

He was not interested in whatever it was but nodded anyway to appease her, and started chewing on his food.

Later that night, he lay on his bed flipping through a photo album when his mother walked in. She sat down beside him and laid a book on his chest. "I found this while I was sorting out your things today. It is Esha's diary. Did you know she kept a diary?" she asked.

She ruffled his hair and turned to leave, saying, "Read it.

I felt much better after I did."

He picked up the diary and flipped through the pages. He soon figured that it was a collection of all her happiest memories, right from the school-bus rides to their wedding day and the life after that. Eagerly, he scanned the pages and felt almost as if Esha was talking to him herself.

I just got back from the best weekend trip ever. I'm so glad Arun suggested for all of us to get together. It was so relaxing and I felt like I was reliving my school days. It made me realise how much I have missed everybody, especially Arun. Spending time with him makes me so happy. It has been so many years, but our special bond is still intact. We can talk about anything. He has not changed at all. He still talks with his mouth full and exclaims how good the food is. We went for a walk on the beach at night and we laughed and splashed each other with water. I can feel my loneliness easing away, whenever I am with him.

He smiled at all the excitement leaping off the pages of her diary. He flipped through some more pages and certain phrases jumped out to him, "*I just want to be with him all the time...*", "*He comes up to me and I feel so safe in his arms...*" and "*The best part is that after fights, he comes and hugs me, takes me in his arms and says, 'Okay, do whatever you want. I will just watch you.' These fights make me want to stay with Arun all the more during holidays.*"

His precious Esha! Reading her words made him feel so much closer to her than he had felt in a long while.

A long entry written over several days caught his eye and he stopped to read it.

Today, I visited the Orphanage after a long time. It felt nice when the kids came running to me. I played all my childhood games with them. They are always so full of joy and happiness that they managed to take away some of my pain too. I've tried my hardest to remember everyone's name.

I saw Anu applying something very gingerly to Radhika's elbows. When I asked her what she was doing, she said very adorably that Radhika's elbows had been aching so she decided to massage them to make her feel better. There was so much care in her voice. I guess her hands must have a healing touch too.

Whenever I hold Anu or make her sit in my lap, I forget about all the worries in the world. She talks all the time and tells me about so many things, as she perceives them. I had never imagined that a simple girl like her could have so many stories. The way she smiles, I feel like hugging her close to my heart and never letting go. I miss her all the time when I am away from her and I can't wait to see her again.

He put the diary on the bedside table and lay back against the pillows. All those orphanage visits and she never once told him about Anu.

The next day, he woke up to her words playing on his mind,

Even now I feel her warmth, as if I am holding her in my

arms. She is a big bundle of happiness for me.

'Who is this girl who had captured Esha's heart?' he wondered. He wished he had gone to visit the orphanage with her sometime. However, it had been clear to him then that Esha needed time to grieve on her own.

His mother turned to look at him as he came into the kitchen to get some coffee. She asked, "Did you read even a little bit?"

He nodded, his mind still stuck on Anu. Thinking aloud, he said, "Perhaps we should go to the orphanage ourselves. Esha talks about this girl Anu a lot. I would like to meet her, I think."

His mother's face broke into a smile, "I thought you might want to go. I have already found out all the details. Shall we go tomorrow?"

He hugged his mother gratefully and said, "Thank you Ma, you always look out for me. I wish Dad was here so that he could come with us too."

"Of course, I am your mother. I have always known what is in your heart, right from the time you were in my womb," she said and ruffled his hair, "I know how you miss your father, but his work requires him to be in Nagpur. He was very unhappy going back when his leave got over."

She set Arun to work chopping vegetables and for once he obliged, his mind preoccupied with the contents of Esha's diary.

When they arrived at the orphanage the next day, he was pleasantly surprised by how peaceful it was. For a moment he just stood there, taking in the view of the large compound surrounded by mango and coconut trees. Alphabets painted across the boundary walls and the playground built in the front evidenced the presence of a lot of kids there.

His mother pointed towards a side entrance to the building from where a few kids emerged, running after each other. A lady came rushing after them, laughing and calling out their names. "These kids make me go nuts," she huffed, walking over to them, "they are always playing and nobody wants to eat on time."

The children gathered around them and giggled. "Come, the food will get cold," she said to them, "If you eat on time, I promise all of you chocolates afterwards."

Quickly, they all became agreeable and ready to follow her back inside.

The lady then asked them, "Have you come to see Father? Please come in and sit. I will let him know you are here."

Gesturing towards the children playing at the swings outside, Arun asked, "Can we wait out here with them?"

"Of course," she said, "I'll just go get him from his office."

He turned to look at his mother with a big smile on his face, the energy and happiness of those children starting to fill his heart already. She smiled back at him and gestured to him to go ahead and interact with the kids.

Stretching on her toes, a little girl was trying to climb on to the swing, but she could not reach it. Arun stepped forward and bent down to help her up. Once she was seated in place, with the chain of the swing tightly clasped in her tiny hands, he gave her a gentle push. She laughed out loud, encouraging him to push harder. He put a little more force into it and watched her swing to and fro happily.

An old man came and stood next to him just then. "Ah, God's little angels. I learn so much from them every time I see them," he said.

Arun observed his long white gown and prayer beads and deduced that he must be the Father. He extended his hand towards him and said, "Father, I am Arun Shetty, Esha's husband…"

The old man interrupted him with a sad sigh and said, "Oh yes, she has told me a lot about you. I was so sorry to hear about her demise. Such a beautiful girl, and so young…I too know the pain of losing someone dear. But my child, when God takes away someone close to us, he gives us the strength to bear the loss too. He gives us pain as well as the strength to fight it."

His mother joined them and put an arm around Arun as he nodded to the Father's words. She said, "You are absolutely correct, Father. Esha always used to say the same thing too."

They made polite introductions before the Father said,

"It is so nice of you to come and visit us. You go ahead and play with the children. They will make you feel much better. I will go make arrangements for some tea."

Arun was not sure how to tell him the reason that had brought them there, but his mother soon spoke up for him. "Father, we actually wanted to meet Anu. Esha had formed a special bond with her and we would like to get to know her as well," she said.

"Anu is a delightful child. I will ask Sister to bring her here. I will be right back," Father said, leaving them alone for a few moments.

A Sister came out with the tea and informed, "Anu is doing her prayers at the moment. She'll be out in five minutes."

Arun's mother took a sip of her tea and gazed lovingly at all the children around her. "Seeing all these little ones reminds me of your childhood days, Arun. You were always running around and playing and I too had to chase after you to make you eat. Then when I'd catch you, you would laugh so cheerfully that I felt as if I was holding the whole world in my arms," she said.

Arun smiled at his mother's words. Just then, the Father appeared from inside the building, leading a small girl by the hand. She had very short hair with a messy fringe, and a broken front tooth where her tongue stuck out when she smiled. She could have been Esha herself in her school days.

"Anu...say hello," the Father encouraged her.

"Hi," Anu said, a little shyly, but flashing a bright smile at them at the same time.

She continued to cling to the Father's hand, even when Arun beckoned her forward. "Go," he said, indicating towards Arun, "They have come to meet you."

Her small glittering eyes and round plump cheeks reminded him of Esha and he felt a sudden pang in his heart for her. She slowly walked closer to him. She had a limp in one leg and took small steps to accommodate for the metal crutches under her arms.

"Hi, I am Arun," he said and kneeled to come to her level of sight.

She crinkled her eyes and put out her free hand towards him, saying, "Hi, I am Anu."

He took her tiny hand in his big one and helped her sit beside him. His mother smiled and reached out to pat her head. Anu looked thrilled to receive so much attention. Forgetting her initial inhibition, she started chatting away about her studies and the games she played, while Arun listened, completely enchanted by her.

His mother had started a conversation with the Father, but Arun had tuned them out, too engrossed in Anu's words. After a while, he felt his mother rest her hand on his arm and heard her say softly, "I have not seen Arun this happy since Esha passed away. This girl is magic."

Chapter 12

The journey back home from the orphanage felt just like the one Arun had in sixth grade, returning home from his first day at school, having made friends with Esha. This time, he spent the long drive chattering away about Anu. He had already started making plans about making another visit so that he could spend more time with her. His mother laughed with glee at the excitement in his voice. Arun felt a smile resting naturally on his face after a long time.

He waited impatiently for a while and finally gave in after a week. “Ma, shall we go visit Anu today? I want to meet her again,” he said, requesting his mother.

Thus, they set out to Sunshine Orphanage on the outskirts of Mumbai once again,. Arun couldn’t tell who was more excited about the visit, Anu or himself. The connection that had sparked between them the first time that they met was lit even brighter by this visit. Both of them laughed and talked with each other throughout the day. She reminded him of Esha so much, with her naughty personality and her ability to instantly put him at ease.

Over the next couple of months, these visits became quite regular. Arun and his mother often made the long drive down to see Anu, and each time they said goodbye, it was as though they were leaving behind a piece of their heart.

On one particular visit, Arun found it harder than usual to leave Anu's company and go home. His mother tried to comfort him saying that they would be back again soon, but he no longer felt content with such fleeting visits. His mother felt deeply his attachment with Anu.

Arun went to the Father and without much of a preamble, he asked, "Can we adopt Anu?"

It was a split second decision and though he could see his mother astounded by his sudden words, he knew in his heart that it was the right thing to do.

Father took a moment to reply, "I am sorry, dear. We are no longer supporting adoption. Last year, a five-year-old girl was adopted by a young couple and when we went there for a procedural audit, we found out that she was being made to do all the household chores. Since that incident, the management had become very cautious and prefers to keep the children here, where they receive proper love and care."

Arun felt his heart break a little and hung his head down

in defeat. Just when he had found a ray of happiness to brighten his darkened life, it was denied to him yet again.

His mother stepped up and holding Anu close to herself, she asked, "For Esha's sake, can't something be done?"

The Father tenderly stroked Anu's cheek and said, "You know, Esha used to be my favourite child and I was very sad to watch her leave. Years later, when Anu was found by the police and brought here, she smiled at me with that same intensity. I feel a similar attachment to her now and do not want to lose her. I know you are good people and she can find a very happy home with you, though. Let me see what I can do. Perhaps the management will permit Anu to stay with you for a few days."

Arun and his mother shared a quick look, happy with the smallest possibility of having more time to spend with Anu. "Thank you, Father. We'll wait here while you speak to them," he said, clutching Anu's hand in his.

A sister came to take Anu inside after a while. Arun waited with his mother, anxiously wondering whether the decision would be in their favour.

His spirits rose when the Father appeared, leading Anu out and carrying a small bag along with. They were followed by a gaggle of children crying and waving at her.

"She is yours for the week," he announced, handing over the bag to Arun. The Father then bent down and said to Anu, "My dear girl, you will love staying with them. And you will be back in a few days. Come on now, who is my good girl?"

Anu sniffled in response, suddenly looking reluctant to leave.

Arun smiled and went forward to encourage her to say goodbye to all her friends.

He heard the Father telling his mother, "I have not told her about Esha yet. Please tell her as and when you and Arun think the time is right."

His mother nodded in acceptance and said, "We will, Father. And don't you worry about Anu, we will take very good care of her."

Arun worried that he was doing Anu wrong by taking her away from all her friends. She sat quietly in the backseat, silent tears running down her cheeks. Although after some time, Anu wiped them away, leaned her crutches against the door and glanced out of the window. They did not speak much, but he kept an eye on her through the rearview mirror, glad with his decision to have taken a cab that day, so that he was free of the need to focus on driving himself.

As he watched, she leaned her head against his mother's shoulder and dozed off. It was late evening by the time they reached home and Anu was fast asleep. He picked her up cautiously, carried her inside and tucked her gently in his bed. He watched her sleep for a long time. Her face was completely peaceful and the small smile that lingered on her face served as a balm for his aching soul. He fell asleep like that, reclining on a sofa nearby.

"Uncle, uncle, wake up!" He heard a tiny voice calling him.

He woke up with a start to see Anu sitting up in bed, looking puzzled. "Good Morning, Anu," he said, "You fell asleep in the car and it was quite late when we reached home so I decided not to wake you. You are at my house now."

He saw that she was not entirely comfortable yet, her eyes scanning the room for something. "Where are my crutches?" she asked, agitated.

He furrowed his brow, trying to recall. He had placed them on the car mat while picking up Anu. He must have left them there, he thought. "Don't worry, I will get them from the car. For now, let me carry you down for breakfast," he said, picking her up in his arms.

He sat her down at the kitchen table and went to call the cab driver, while his mother cooed and fussed over Anu.

The driver apologised saying that he would only be able to come by evening, so Anu had to spent the day in his arms. This made them both very happy. Arun swung her up and she held him tightly around the neck. Her laughter and giggles made even Rambo spring up with a renewed life. He jumped around them, wagged his tail, and barked.

For the first time since Esha's death, an aura of happiness shimmered around them. Even his mother played with them and insisted on giving Anu a bath in the evening. Anu demanded that she be carried around even though she now had her crutches back.

He held her small body close to his and took her to the tub, which his mother had filled with warm water. He watched how tenderly and carefully his mother bathed her, as if Anu were her own grandchild already. She massaged her with oil, dressed her, and put a dot of Kohl at her neck to ward off the evil eye.

It was when they took her to pray that she spotted Esha's photo kept next to the idols of Gods. She examined the photo with her childish curiosity and Arun felt a lump form in his throat. His mother put her arm around Anu and told her, "Esha aunty is in heaven with God now."

He could not stand to watch Anu crying in his mother's arms and slipped away to his room to go through Esha's photographs by himself.

A little while later, Anu limped into the room. She crawled up onto the bed and came to sit close to Arun, a solemn expression on her face. Without saying anything, she flipped through the pages of the album, patiently observing the details in each photograph.

He was touched by her attempt to console him in his sadness.

"Anu, let us go and have dinner. It has been a long day for you, you must take rest," said Arun, giving a soft pat on her head.

Anu asked, "Can I finish my writing first and then go for dinner?"

Arun nodded his head in a yes. Anu quickly reached for her bag, pulled out a notebook and started scribbling something on it. Arun enquired what she was writing, to which she replied, "Father always asks us to write in a book, whatever you feel happy about and then read it when you are sad or feeling alone."

Arun remembered Esha doing the same thing in her diary. He determined to start writing and recording all his wonderful experiences with Anu in Esha's diary.

Anu had already created a special place in his heart. She reminded him of the simple things that Esha used to engage with in her daily life, like feeding the birds, writing a gratitude journal, praying or feeling happy about all the small things in life. He often wondered how even the routine things from everyday became so exciting with Esha and Anu around. He felt Anu to be just like Esha; simple, yet different.

Arun's mother wholeheartedly supported Arun's new relationship. For that entire week, she was always at hand to feed Anu and help give her a bath. Arun started to join them in the prayer room. While his mother taught Anu about the mantras and how to light the lamp, he would keep his eyes closed and pray for Anu's happiness.

After lunch, Anu would join them for a stroll on the

beach and play games with them.

On the third night, Arun sat beside Anu and narrated a bedtime story to her. As she drifted off to sleep, he reflected on how quickly she had managed to change his life. He was due to start his new job as a hotel manager the next day, and it was all because of Anu that he had finally listened to his mother and applied in the first place.

He found it hard to imagine working at the hotel, while Anu playing in the sand with his mother and Rambo.

When Arun went to work the next day, he watched Anu wave and greet all of his hotel staff and ask them how they were? She had already made friends with many of them. That evening, when he sat down with her after winding down from work, she discussed with him her new friends and told him all about their families too.

Arun was touched by Anu's compassion and observational skills. She had clearly noted each person's behavior, their activities and enquired tender-heartedly about their families as well.

Arun learnt a beautiful lesson that day. A simple smile and a few gently words of compassion can bring so much happiness to another person's life.

Each day, Anu taught Arun a small yet significant thing about life.

One day, Anu was playing with Rambo, who was having

fun barking at and chasing away birds from the deck chairs next to the hotel pool. Anu limped behind Rambo, trying to get to him to stop, when Rambo made a sudden excited leap and knocked Anu into the pool.

Arun's mother jumped up in alarm, immediately signalling the life guard. Without wasting another moment, Arun leapt out of his seat before the lifeguard could make a move and dove in after Anu. She flailed her arms and legs about frantically, gripping her arms tightly around his neck when he reached her. Even when he had caught her and held her head safely above the surface, she continued to move her legs underwater.

He carried her out of the pool and stood watching as she spat out the water she had swallowed.

"Are you okay?" he asked, concern etched on his face.

Anu nodded and immediately launched into describing what had just happened. He half listened to her, his attention suddenly taken by how she had been able to move her leg so easily under water. He touched her stiff leg and asked, "What has happened to your leg, Anu? Why can't you walk properly?"

Anu replied, "Father told me that I once had a high fever when I was three years old and since then my leg has been like this. The doctors could not figure out why it happened and gave crutches to help me walk."

She looked down at her leg, accustomed to how it had

always been for her. Arun, however, was determined to do something for her and promised, "We will find another doctor and see if it can be fixed, okay? Now, do you want to go into the water again?"

Anu looked terrified at the thought, "But what if I can't move my leg and drown?"

"I will be there to hold you," he replied. He got into the pool and held her horizontally at the surface of water to help her float. His heart danced with joy with every small move and splash Anu made.

He bought her to work every day for the rest of that week, and watched her become more and more confident in the water.

When the time came for her to return to the orphanage, he felt sick with the thought of not having her around all the time anymore. He held Anu close to himself for the entire journey back and she sat subdued in his arms.

However, as they neared the orphanage, Anu brightened considerably at the thought of meeting her friends again.

She went running to hug the Father around the middle when they finally reached and talked his ear off all the way to his office. Arun sat down with his mother, feeling light and happy, listening to the excitement with which Anu described her time with them.

He found it very difficult to leave that day and kept

turning back for one last hug. With Anu gone, emptiness filled their house once again. He continued his new job, but often found himself rooted to the spot, his gaze drawn to the pool or the beach, where he had spent so much time playing with Anu.

He knew that he had his mother worried with his apathy. Finally, she suggested that they start to visit Anu every weekend again. The distance between them fell away with every visit and he came to realise the truth of Esha's words, "She is just a small package with tons of happiness."

On one such visit, when they were about to leave, Anu threw her arms around his neck and started crying.

"I'll be back next week," he promised, feeling helpless.

But she clung to him, unwilling to let go. Arun turned to the Father standing nearby and asked him to hold Anu. He stepped forward and spoke directly to Anu. He asked, "Anu, do you want to stay with Uncle?"

She stopped crying at once and nodded her head assertively. Arun's own breathing quickened at the prospect and he looked at the Father expectantly.

"Yes," the Father smiled, answering the unasked question, "I have been talking to the management regarding Anu's adoption. There is a possibility that we can make it work on special grounds."

Arun almost jumped with joy. He held Anu closer to him

and listened carefully.

"But it will be a long process," the Father continued, "First, we need to obtain their approval to permit the adoption. After that, there will be a lot of paperwork, submitting proofs and getting the verification done by the adoption authorities. It is a long, tedious process."

Arun turned to his mother for support and they both nodded gravely. His mother asked, "Will Anu be able to stay with us while the paperwork is being processed?"

"Not yet," he replied, "She will have to stay here till we get the management's permission at least. We should know their decision in another week. Once that is done, you can submit the paperwork and take her home. However, I must warn you that it isn't for certain that your request will be approved by the adoption authorities. If they don't approve it, there is nothing we'll be able to do, thereafter. "

Arun turned to Anu and said, "Only a few days more, Anu, then you can come and stay with us forever. We won't have to say goodbye anymore."

It was a short, impatient wait, but Anu soon came home with them and changed their lives irrevocably.

Epilogue

One day, Arun returned from work to find an unknown car parked outside his house. The sound of people talking and laughing drifted out of the sitting room and he wondered curiously as to who the visitors might be.

He hurried inside and the scene in front of him made him freeze in his tracks. Esha's parents sat with Anu, lovingly listening to her story while his mother and Rohit watched them.

He cleared his throat audibly from the doorway and everybody turned to look at him.

Esha's father stood up and approached him nervously. He said, "Arun, you must understand that Esha was the most priceless possession for me. Once she came home, there was nothing left to ask God for. But then, she disobeyed me and choose to marry you. I always believed that since I had brought her up, I had the complete prerogative to decide her future for her. It never occurred to me that she had all the right to choose her own partner, the person she wanted to spend her life with. It took me a long time to realise my mistake. I am so sorry, son. I just wanted her to be happy."

He took a deep breath and continued, "She died before we could make amends, and I did not have the courage to come and meet you."

Arun was nonplussed. He held out his hand in comfort towards Esha's father. Rohit spoke up from the other side of the room, "I met Uncle at his clinic the other day and he asked after you. When I told him about Anu, he insisted that we make this trip to Goa to meet you."

Esha's mother gently caressed Anu's cheeks and said, "Looking at this girl makes me feel like I am seeing Esha again. I am so glad that we decided to come. I hope we can put the past behind us. We too would like to be a part of Anu's life."

Arun smiled through his tears and said, "I would not have it any other way. You must stay and have dinner with us."

'Esha was right,' he thought, 'she knew that a child would melt their hearts.' It was sad, however, that she lived no more to see it, but with Anu in his life, he felt slightly healed of Esha's loss.

After dinner, he brought Anu forward and said to Esha's father, "You are a renowned orthopaedic doctor. Please take a look at Anu's leg. She can neither feel it, nor walk properly on it, but she is like a fish in the water."

He told him about the swimming pool incident and held Anu's hand as Esha's father examined her leg. After some tapping, pinching, and probing, he asked Anu to stand up without the support of her crutches. Anu stood up promptly, but as soon as she put her weight on her right leg, it buckled and she slopped down on the couch.

Arun watched him twist each part of her leg and press her foot hard, eliciting a scream out of her. "Ah…that hurts, please stop," she cried.

Finally, Esha's father stood up and turning to face the room, he said, "She still has some sensation in her leg. We have hope…Arun, bring her to my clinic soon and we will start with the treatment right away."

He put on his coat in preparation to leave, while Esha's mother bent down and slipped two beaded bangles of gold onto Anu's wrists.

Anu turned her hands over to watch the bangles dance and said, "These are so pretty!"

Esha's mother smiled and said, "I was supposed to gift these to Esha on her wedding day. They were her favourite. Now, they are yours."

Anu hugged her tightly and whispered, "Thank you,

Aunty. This means a lot."

With the promise to come back again soon, Esha's parents left. Anu had quickly grown attached to them, Arun noticed with a smile. She was the most friendly and affectionate little girl he had ever met.

Excited about the possibility of her leg being treated, he enrolled her for swimming classes the very next day. But even as it was, her leg worked so well under water that she swam faster than most of the other children there.

Her instructor soon took notice of her skills and suggested entering her name in the kids swimming championship to Arun. Anu was dedicated and practised hard for her first competition.

On the day of the event, Arun woke up early to get Anu ready and say their prayers. He packed the necessary items for the competition and they reached the crowded venue in time. He kneeled to face her and said, "Whether you win or lose today, you are always a champion for me."

It was important to him that Anu understood that. He knew it was something that Esha would have said to her too. Anu smiled and reached out to hug him, her hands barely reaching around his shoulders.

Together they got her band and number, and then walked over to the starting blocks. He felt completely at ease with her, just like the other parents present there, fussing over her swimming cap and making sure that she was ready. Being

Anu's parent came naturally to him.

He then made his way to the other end of the pool. He stood next to his mother and watched the race closely. The whistle blew and Anu was off like a shot. She kicked her legs and swam furiously, gaining speed and cutting across the water. He waited for her at the finish line and as soon as she reached the end, he quickly lifted her out of the pool.

She had not come first, but while he wrapped a towel around her and rubbed her hair to dry it, he noticed a satisfied smile on her face.

When the winners were announced, Anu was given a special prize for a brilliant performance despite her disability. People gathered around her and asked, "How do you manage to swim so fast? Are you not scared of the water at all?"

Anu replied shyly, "My Papa was standing at the opposite end. I just saw him and swam as fast as I could to reach him."

He laughed along with everyone else at her innocent answer and clapped proudly. He was moved by her love and the way she referred to him as Papa. Arun hugged Anu tightly and lifted her up in the air.

Arun's mother stood beside them with tears in her eyes. At that moment, she felt at peace and thanked Esha's soul for giving Arun a purpose in life again.

When they said love is pure and unique
They didn't mean it to be only for a man and a woman
It belongs to everyone on this planet
As the sun never discriminates over giving its light to a specific place
So is love; it is needed by everyone
When your heart weeps for the loss of a loved one
Search for someone who is longing for love just like you
You may not find what you've lost, but you might just become the reason for someone else's smile and love.

This story is a work of fiction and should not be construed otherwise. It does not seek to invalidate any procedural requirements or operable laws of India, especially in the matter of Adoption. The author is aware that as per the law at the time of writing the novel, a single male is not permitted to adopt a girl child. She presents this story in an alternative reality, and it may only be accepted as an argument to the extent that a more flexible legal framework, which operates based on the facts and circumstances of each case, might have the possibility of changing many lives for the better.